JY '97

Twilight in Grace Falls

A Richard Jackson Book

Twilight in Grace Falls

Natalie Honeycutt

Orchard Books   New York

8997538

Orchard Books, 95 Madison Avenue,
New York, NY 10016

Manufactured in the United States of America
Book design by Mina Greenstein
The text of this book is set in 12 point Sabon.
10 9 8 7 6 5 4 3 2 1

Library of Congress Cataloging-in-Publication Data

Honeycutt, Natalie.
Twilight in Grace Falls / Natalie Honeycutt.
    p. cm.
"A Richard Jackson book."
Summary: Eleven-year-old Dasie watches the effects on
her family and friends when the lumber mill that
supports the town closes its doors.
ISBN 0-531-30007-2. ISBN 0-531-33007-9 (lib. bdg.)
[1. Lumbermen—Fiction. 2. Lumber and lumbering—
Fiction. 3. Family life—Fiction. 4. Death—
Fiction. 5. Grief—Fiction. 6. Logging—Fiction.]
I. Title.
PZ7.H7467 Tw 1997
[Fic]—dc20   96-42388

FOR ROD,
with all my heart

Twilight in Grace Falls

one

The sky above Grace Falls was cast over with an eerie orange haze, and the spicy-sweet smell of wood smoke hung thick in the air. The smell was right for October, when the first fires of the season were lit in woodstoves all over town. But this wasn't October. It was late August.

Dasie pushed open the screen door, letting her brother's dog, Tattler, onto the back porch. She followed him, barefoot and still in her nightgown, down the steps and into the yard. It had been almost three hours since the beeping of the pager echoed from the kitchen, rousing them all from bed.

"Attention, Grace Falls fire personnel. There is a reported fire at the Grace Falls Lumber Company. Attention, Grace Falls fire personnel. . . ."

Within moments light had shone from the kitchen down the short back hall to Dasie's bedroom.

She heard the familiar squawk and pop of the utility closet door followed by two firm clomps as her father shoved his feet into his boots, then a grunt as he hauled up the heavy pants of his turnouts.

Dasie had groped for a sweatshirt and pulled it on over her nightgown. She arrived in the kitchen in time to see her dad take his helmet from her mother's hand, clap it onto his head, and start for the door. The chin strap still dangled as he spoke into his hand-held radio: "Captain six-oh-four responding."

"You be careful, Hank Jenson," Dasie's mom called after him.

He lifted a hand in a backward wave and strode quickly across the lawn to the gate. Seconds later the wheels of his pickup splattered gravel as he pulled away into the night.

"Anybody seen my keys?"

Dasie turned. Her brother, Sam, eighteen, stood fully dressed in the doorway between the kitchen and the dining room. He patted his jeans pockets as he scanned the surfaces of the kitchen.

"Now, Sam, you don't need to be going," their mother said.

"Mom, it's the *mill*." He turned as though to head back through the dining room and the hall to the two front bedrooms.

Dasie lifted a folded copy of the *Morgantown Weekly* from the kitchen counter and picked up Sam's keys. "They're right here," she said.

Sam grinned and ran a hand upward through

Dasie's hair. "Thanks, kid," he said. He paused just long enough to peck their mother on the cheek, then pushed through the back door. His pickup truck whined and stalled before the engine caught a steady beat, and he, too, pulled away, turning north at the corner.

Dasie and her mother stood at the screen door, Tattler between them.

"I wish he'd get that taillight fixed," her mother said. "He said he wouldn't drive at night until he did."

"He'll be okay," Dasie said. She knew her mother wasn't really worried about the taillight. Sam wasn't on the volunteer fire department. The only other time he'd gone on a call was when the Baxter place burned, during last winter's bad storm, and her father thought they might need extra hands for clearing snow.

The *mill.* Sam had been right. The lumber mill north of town was where their father went to work every day. It was where at least one person from every third house in Grace Falls went to work every day. Grace Falls was a mill town. Even if your family didn't work there, chances were you still depended on the mill for a living. One way or another, almost everyone did.

As Dasie and her mother watched, another set of headlights briefly swept the intersection, headed north. That would be Danny Cabrini from down on First Street. He'd be the last firefighter from their end of town.

Dasie knew them all. She often baby-sat for Chief Raines's three children. Then there was the assistant chief, Polly Ware, who'd grown up next door to her father and whose daughter, Amy, had just graduated from Grace Falls High School with Sam. Even her cousin Warren, one year older than Sam, was in the department. Each of them would be headed toward the mill. Or there already.

CONSOLIDATED TIMBER PRODUCTS. INC. That's how it read in bright blue lettering on the sign in front. "Why did the pager say 'Grace Falls Lumber Company'?" Dasie had asked her mother. "Nobody calls it that anymore."

"Not for the last twenty years," her mother agreed. "But a lot of folks will never think of it as anything else." With a shiver she pulled her light cotton robe close at the neck. "Mother Grace," she murmured.

Dasie had run her fingers through the thick thatch of fur between Tattler's shoulders. "Is it bad?" she asked.

"I don't know, Dasie. I'm standing here telling myself there's sprinklers through every inch of that mill. I can't think how a fire could even start."

It was then they had first smelled smoke.

Her mother sprinted to the dining room and the radio scanner on top of the bookcase. For nearly three hours, she sat as Dasie had so often seen her— huddled into the corner of the old flowered sofa, her knees drawn up to her chin, listening.

Dasie, restless, wandered about the room. It was

home to all of their oldest and most comfortable furniture, and Dasie liked it just as it was; she did not share her mother's yearning for a formal dining table of polished wood. She sat sometimes in the overstuffed chair across from the wood stove, then, as day slowly dawned, stood more often by the window.

All the while, the scanner crackled with familiar voices. But most of what they said was in code. Dasie and her mother knew only that the fire was too large for the Grace Falls department to handle alone. The chief had called for "mutual aid," and a truck had arrived from Morgantown, some eighteen miles distant over the mountain pass. The small city of Faro, still farther away, had a truck on the way.

Now, in the backyard, Dasie studied the smudgy sky. It was impossible to tell how big the fire really was. Or even exactly what was burning. What she wanted to do, suddenly, was get on her bike and pedal up to the mill. She could be there in ten minutes, even less.

She left Tattler nosing around the edge of the fence and went back inside. From the dining room she could hear her mother talking to someone on the phone.

"Yes, but Warren's just a rookie, Betsy. Rookies are never given dangerous assignments. . . . But even so, Hank's there. You know he'll look after Warren. Really, Bets, you don't need to worry."

That settled it. If her mother was talking to Aunt

Betsy, and if the subject was her cousin Warren, this call would take a while. Dasie could get to the mill and back before she was hardly missed. She'd find Sam and her father, see for herself what was going on.

In her bedroom she changed quickly into a pair of shorts and a T-shirt. For a moment she stood with her sweatshirt in hand, trying to decide. By ten o'clock it would be hot. But it was still cool now. She put the sweatshirt back on, picked up her hairbrush, and tugged quickly through her shoulder-length brown hair. Then she pulled on her ball cap and gathered her hair and stuffed it out the hole in back. She frowned at the image in the mirror.

At eleven-going-on-twelve, Dasie had lately been growing in one direction. Up. Her parents spoke of it as spindling up. But whatever they called it, Dasie hoped it would quit soon. She didn't want to wind up like Sam—six foot two.

Dasie tied the laces of her high-tops, made her way back through the kitchen, and stood at the dining-room door until her mother looked her way.

"Back soon," Dasie said, and waved.

"Oh, Dasie. Uh, just a minute, Bets."

But by then Dasie was outside. She wheeled her bike through the gate, leaving Tattler, with his wagging tail and beseeching eyes, behind.

The mill road wound through tall stands of ponderosa pine, then opened out to the wide expanse of mill property. All along the road stood stack after stack, row upon row of finished lumber, all neatly wrapped and waiting for shipment.

Dasie squinted into the morning sun, finding first the outline of the vast planing mill building against the sky. To the left, from somewhere past sight, rose a spreading column of smoke. As she neared the mill entry, Dasie passed cars and trucks parked on either side of the road. Clumps of her neighbors stood at anxious watch.

It wasn't hard to find Sam. He was in front of the wide mill gate, feet planted, arms folded. Parked. His pickup truck was parked nearby.

"Yo!" he said.

"How bad is it?" Dasie asked.

"Bad enough. What are you doing here?"

"I just want to know what's going on," she said. "There's so much smoke. Is it the sawmill?"

"No, a log deck. Two of them, in fact."

In the mill yard, raw logs were stacked in decks from fifty to two hundred yards long, forty to fifty feet high. Logs by the thousands, piled up like so many matchsticks. How much of it would burn? Some? All?

Dasie followed Sam's gaze down the dirt-and-gravel road, past the planing mill building, where it curved out of sight.

"Can I go in?" she asked. "I won't get in the way."

"No. Sorry, but I'm supposed to keep everyone out. It's a cooker, Dasie. And there's so much equipment in there—trucks from the Forest Service, Morgantown, you name it."

"Where's Dad?"

Sam lowered his head, then raised it and looked again along the gravel road. "In there," he said.

"Is he okay?"

Sam's eyes narrowed. Watching him, Dasie saw how his hair still stood in spikes of sleep, like someone leaning sideways to a wind.

"Sam?"

He shook his head. "He's okay, Dasie. You know he's okay."

Dasie did know. Just as soon as Sam said it, she knew. After all, just yesterday—wasn't it only yesterday?—she'd watched her father out by their woodshed as he stood at one end of an even row of log rounds. He raised his maul, then brought it down with a *thwack*, neatly splitting the first round. Then he walked easily down the entire row. *Thwack. Thwack. Thwack.* He split each round with just one stroke, and when he reached the end, he was breathing hard and laughing at the same time. He laughed with the sun sparkling off his deep mahogany hair, making little glints that looked for all the world like stars. "I'd like to do that all over again," he said.

Nothing could happen to a father who had stars in his hair and who laughed at the very moment he'd worn himself out. Of this, Dasie was certain.

"How's Mom holding up?" Sam asked.

"Okay," Dasie said. "I mean, you know. She's

Mom. She's been glued to the scanner. She's starting to get worried 'cause she hasn't heard Dad for a while."

A muscle twitched along Sam's jaw, but when he didn't speak, Dasie went on. "It's not just Dad. It's Polly, too. It's been maybe an hour since we heard either of them, so she's about decided they're together. And she's starting to think they're up to something."

"You shouldn't have left her alone," Sam said. "You know how she is when Dad's at a fire."

Inwardly, Dasie sagged. She knew better—*had* known better—than to leave their mother alone. "She was on the phone with Aunt Betsy, though. She hardly noticed I left."

"Betsy?" Sam rolled his eyes. "Let me guess. Betsy's worried about Warren, right?"

"That's what it sounded like," Dasie said.

"Huh. Now there's a career opportunity. You're right, Mom'll be tied up for a while."

No matter where they began, her mother's conversations with Aunt Betsy never seemed to end until they'd traveled the same ground. First they'd skirt around how well Warren got along with Uncle Frank—or didn't—and then they'd come to the heart of it: the trouble with Warren, and who was to blame.

Dasie herself had no idea what was wrong with Warren, or whether, for that matter, there *was* something wrong. But a little more than two years earlier, in the spring of his junior year, Warren

9

up and quit high school. A giant ruckus had followed. For days, weeks, Warren was the stubborn center of a family storm while Aunt Betsy, Uncle Frank, and Dasie's parents tried to change his mind.

They kept at him until the day Sam lost his temper. "You're just *tormenting* Warren," he said to his parents. "You, Betsy, Frank, even Grandma, you talk like you never even met him. Warren was never going to finish school. Couldn't you *see* that?" As much as anything, Dasie thought her parents were astonished—Sam never got angry. But after that they fell silent on the subject of Warren and school.

From down the mill road came the deep blast of an air horn. Dasie and Sam turned to see a fire truck headed their way—a truck nearly twice as long as either of the Grace Falls engines and equipped with a cherry picker.

"It's the engine from Faro," Sam said. He pushed the big iron gate aside in a wide arc.

Dasie counted six firefighters as the truck slowed to an idle beside them.

"This the way?" the driver asked.

"Straight ahead for about three hundred yards," Sam said, "then the road will curve to your left. It'll take you right into the log yard."

As the truck lumbered away, Dasie breathed, "Wow."

"Pretty impressive, huh? If Grace Falls had a rig like that, we'd have to build a new hall."

While they stood watching the receding fire truck, Dasie spotted a familiar small silver pickup coming from the opposite direction.

"Is that Amy?"

"Looks like it," Sam said.

"You let Amy in but not your own sister? I wouldn't call that fair." Not that Dasie really minded. Amy Ware and Sam had gone to their senior prom together—for the fun of it, they said, just as friends—and Dasie would never forget seeing them that night. Sam was so splendid in a western-cut tux and Amy so breathtaking in a slinky peach gown that since then Dasie'd spend hours imagining their wedding, once Sam got back from the Navy. She planned to be a bridesmaid.

"It's not about fairness," Sam said. "It's about food. Amy rounded up a couple of coffee urns and the entire stock of doughnuts from Sophie's. Fuel for the troops."

Amy pulled abreast of them and leaned out the window. Her nose was freckled and peeling from working all summer in the mill yard. "Look who's here," she said, smiling at Dasie.

"How's it going back there?" Sam asked.

"They've got their hands full," she said seriously. "The fire's barely contained. If a wind comes up, we'll be in real trouble."

"Did you see my dad?" Dasie asked.

"Yeah. He's partnered up with my mom," Amy said. "As usual."

A look passed between Sam and Amy, and he

gave a small shake of his head. Something about it made Dasie uneasy.

Amy touched her fingers to her lips, then said, "Tell you what, Dasie. I'm on my way down to the Gifford house to see if they'll open the market early so I can pick up some cinnamon rolls and maybe a couple of pies. Those doughnuts disappeared soon as they got there. Why don't you throw your bike in the back and ride along with me?"

Dasie was tempted but shook her head. "I'd better not. I told Mom I'd be back soon."

Sam reached out and tugged at the bill of her cap. "Good girl," he said. "And try to keep her away from the scanner if you can."

"I'll try," Dasie said. "But no promises. It's you Mom listens to, not me."

"That's just because I'm older," Sam said. "But that'll all change as soon as I leave. You'll see."

Dasie brushed a lock of hair from her cheek. Even though she knew that in just two weeks Sam would be gone, it didn't seem real. No more real than that something might happen to her father. She turned back once more toward the billowing cloud of smoke, then left for home.

Her mother stood at the stove, pouring coffee from a fresh pot. She hadn't changed from her nightgown and robe. Tattler lay under the kitchen table, resting one eye at a time.

"I was just hoping you'd get back," Dasie's mom said. "Honestly, I thought I'd never get Betsy off the phone. And then I no sooner hung up than Grandma Jenson called. Did you see your father?"

"No, just Sam. And Amy for a minute. They're not letting anyone in." Dasie, suddenly famished, opened a cupboard and pulled down a jar of peanut butter. She dropped two pieces of bread in the toaster.

Her mother walked to the sink and looked out the window at the murky sky. "This smoke! It only seems to get worse. And I can't make heads or tails of what they're saying on the scanner. As soon as I think I know what's going on, I start to think I don't."

"Well, all I know is it's a couple of log decks."

"Log decks," her mother mused. Then, almost under her breath, she said, "Don't be a hero, Hank. It's just wood. You don't have to save it."

Dasie knew there was no such thing as "just" wood to her dad. He'd never stand to see a stick of it wasted. Not if he could help it.

Her mother wandered with her coffee cup back to the dining room. Dasie slathered the toast with peanut butter, then called, "Do you want a soft-boiled egg, Mom? I could fix it while you get dressed."

"I don't think so, Dasie. I'm not really hungry." She stood next to the scanner, staring at it. Almost coaxing, it seemed. "What I really want is to know where your father is. Him and Polly, both."

"Well, Amy says they're partnered up."

"Those two!" her mother said. "*Children* have more sense."

And then, as if to prove her right, the scanner crackled to life: "*Six-oh-five, tell those men to keep their hoses down! They almost knocked a man off this deck! GET THOSE HOSES DOWN!*"

He didn't identify himself. He didn't have to. It was Hank Jenson. There was a quick blur of yelling, then the radio fell silent.

Dasie's mother turned. Her eyes were wide. "They're up on those decks? Oh, Dasie . . ."

For a moment Dasie felt light-headed. That towering column of smoke, the burning log decks. It wasn't possible that anyone could be on top.

And yet. Her memory reeled through other fires. Times when her father and Polly were first inside a burning house, first on a smoldering roof. If a blazing log deck needed firefighters on top, Polly and her father would be there.

Her mother sank to the dining room sofa with a look Dasie had seen before. There'd be no moving her now, Dasie knew, until the fire was out.

two

When Dasie next heard her father's voice, it was almost noon: *"Six-oh-one, six-oh-four, as soon as Polly's done checking for hot spots, I think we're clear to bring that loader in here on the east end."* After that it seemed every third word over the scanner came from him, as though he wanted his whereabouts known. And perhaps he did.

Her mother was suddenly charged with energy. She showered, dressed, then ripped a piece of paper off a pad and slapped it on the kitchen table. *Menu,* she scrawled across the top, and under that a list: *corn bread, salad, pork ribs, fried squash, potato salad, corn on the cob, deviled eggs, baked beans, lemon cake, and ice cream.* Each, Dasie noted, was a favorite of her father's. He'd probably be surprised to have them all at once.

By late afternoon cooking projects were spread from one side of the kitchen to the other. Dasie was peeling eggs for the potato salad, and her mother mixing a batter for fried summer squash, when the screen door slammed behind Sam. Tattler was all over him, jumping and circling.

"What's all this?" Sam asked. "We expecting company?"

"Not that I had planned," their mother said. Then she looked around and laughed. "It is rather a lot, isn't it? I guess I thought you fellows would be hungry after working so hard all day." She tilted her head up at Sam. "You tired?" she asked.

"Not me," Sam said. "Dad's the one to be tired. He's still working mop-up. It'll be a while."

"That's okay. He doesn't have to do anything when he gets here except rest." She smiled at Sam. "You're sunburned."

"Not much," he said. "The hardest work I did was traffic control. Mostly it was turning away gawkers."

"I don't see what's wrong with gawking," Dasie said. "Usually half the town turns out for a fire. And it's not only gawking, Sam. People help if they can."

"I know that," Sam said. "It's just that today was different. Everyone wanted to go in, but there was so much equipment in that log yard it's a wonder any of 'em got out again."

Their mother turned from the counter, the dripping whisk poised in her hand. "I can still hardly believe it," she said. "How did it start? Do they know yet?"

"Well, the last I spoke to Dad, they were thinking

maybe spontaneous combustion." He pulled off his ball cap and hung it on the rack by the door. "It's this heat, and then there are wood chips and sawdust under those decks."

"And your father? Did he and Polly—"

"Uh, look," Sam interrupted, "do you need any help here? 'Cause if you don't, I thought I'd grab a shower."

"Oh!" she said. "Oh, no, we're fine. Thanks, Sam, you go ahead."

Dasie glanced at his retreating back, knowing he'd deliberately dodged their mother's questions. But Anne Jenson gave no sign of noticing. She wiped her hands and gathered up a grocery list and several bills from her wallet. She handed them to Dasie. "Do you mind, Dasie? We only need five things. I'd like to stay here and finish up."

"Sure," Dasie said. She'd had enough of the kitchen, and a trip to the market meant a chance to run into friends.

"And if you could collect the mail, too?" her mother asked.

Dasie stopped first at the post office, edging her way past a knot of three or four people who stood in the doorway, mail in hand, discussing the fire.

Farther down Main Street, Gifford's Market fairly buzzed with talk. In every aisle a shopping cart or two was parked haphazardly, abandoned while news was exchanged. Dasie dawdled her way through, listening to scraps of this and that. Sometimes she thought most of what she knew in this world came from listening in on other people's conversations.

At the vegetable counter she ran into her best friend, Monica. Both were there for fresh corn, and Monica shifted from one foot to another, her brown eyes flashing with excitement. "Did you hear it's going to be on the Channel Six news tonight?" she said. "Supposedly they got pictures of the chief and your dad and Polly Ware and a few other people."

"No kidding!" Dasie said. She'd never seen Grace Falls on the news before. It was hard to find even on a map. And her father? That would be something.

She followed Monica to the checkout counter. Becky Hodges rang up the groceries and said, "I hear the Grace Falls Fire Department did themselves proud today. You tell your dad for us that we're all grateful, okay?"

Dasie hardly felt her feet as she walked home up First Street. The sky was clear now, returned to a brilliant August blue, and the air had a shimmering quality. It seemed to her that Grace Falls had never been prettier. As she passed the Cabrini house, she saw Danny's turnouts spread over his front hedge, drying in the sun. The sight of them filled her with pride.

Then, at the corner of Cedar Street, she caught sight of her house. It was just like most of the other houses in town, small and square with a steep pitched roof. "Mill housing," her mother would say, in a way that made it sound like less than it should be. But Dasie liked the way it fit in, the belonging look it had, and she especially liked it in summer, when petunias bloomed in the window boxes, her parents' prized chrysanthemums grew tall inside the fence, and black-eyed Susans grew wild outside.

Spread over the fence not one but two sets of turnouts were drying in the sun. Her father's were old and faded, the reflective stripes dimmed with the ash of a hundred fires. The other pair, Warren's, were new and bright, almost sparkling. Warren's turnouts, Dasie decided, had intentions.

Sam and Warren were in the side yard, loading charcoal into the grill. "One of you guys could open the gate!" she called.

"Hey!" Warren said, and covered the distance to the gate in loping strides. He took the larger sack of groceries from her arms and peered into the top. "Gee, Dasie, did you leave any pork ribs for anyone else?"

"Talk to Mom," Dasie said. "It was her list. But you should hear the talk at the market."

Sam groaned. "Uh-oh, the *Daily News*. I can just imagine."

"No, really, Sam. Everyone's talking about the fire. I heard someone say the fire marshal has to investigate. And Monica's afraid old Horace Perkins might lose his job as night watchman 'cause someone said he was sleeping. Is that true?"

"The fire marshal always investigates a fire this

size," Sam said. "And as for Horace Perkins, he's worked at that mill for fifty years with an unblemished record. He made every clock on time, Dasie."

"If it hadn't been for Horace, we might have lost the whole plant," Warren added. He took the second sack of groceries and headed for the back door.

"Tell Mom the mail's in the bottom of the sack," Dasie called. "So's the change."

Warren soon returned with soft drinks, a dishcloth, and a vase and a pair of pruners, which he handed to Dasie. "Your mother says would you kindly cut some flowers for the picnic table. I said I'd do it, but she didn't seem to think I was equal to the job."

"She just doesn't want your big feet tramping through her flower bed," Dasie said. Then she remembered. "Were you up on a log deck today, Warren? Someone said at the market you were."

"Not me." Warren smiled. "I'm a peon. I got to hold a hose, though. That was something."

"Well, I guess Channel Six news got pictures of the fire and of people on top of the decks. Which probably means Dad. And Polly, too. It's supposed to be on the seven-o'clock news tonight."

"Just keep that under your hat," Sam said.

"So Mom won't hear?" Dasie shook her head, disbelieving. "It's too late," she said. "Mom already figured out he was up there. And even if she hadn't, it's all over town!"

"But she didn't hear it from *us*, Dasie. And anyhow, there's a world of difference between knowing something and seeing it with your own eyes. Plus, we promised Dad." Then Sam took a long draft of his soda and looked off toward the south, where blue-green mountains rimmed the horizon. He seemed to be considering something. Finally he said, "What I think Dad's really worried about is if she gets the idea the fire department is too dangerous, she might make him quit."

Dasie sucked in her breath. "Do you really think she'd do that? I mean, Dad loves the department!"

"Yeah, but, Dasie— Well, you were probably too young to remember, but once Mom decided logging was too dangerous, she nagged at Dad for years. That's why he quit logging and took the job at the mill. He finally gave up."

"But that was only because Uncle John got killed!" Dasie protested.

As soon as she'd spoken, she regretted it. "Oh, Warren, I'm sorry. I never meant to say—"

"That's okay," Warren said quickly. "I mean, I was so little when Dad died, I barely remember him. No big deal, you know?" He swatted the edge of the table with the dishcloth and didn't really look at anyone.

"Still," Dasie said, "I shouldn't have." Lordy. Nobody talked about Warren's father. Ever. Almost ever. And certainly not in front of Warren.

What Dasie knew she had pieced together— *gleaned,* really, from bits and scraps of conversations over the years. Scraps that only began to form themselves into a kind of sense in her mind when she was nearing ten years old. By then, of course, it was long after the fact. Or facts. The fact of an uncle, her father's brother, who had died before she was born. And the fact of her aunt Betsy's remarriage to a man whose real name was Ray, though her father dubbed him the First Man, meaning "the first man who came along."

The First Man stayed for eight years. He couldn't seem to hold a job longer than a few months, and the way he told it, the fault always lay with someone else. And he had a temper he took with him to a bar in Morgantown and brought home ugly.

Dasie's father never referred to "when Betsy and Ray got divorced." Instead he spoke of it as "when Betsy finally got rid of the First Man," making it clear he'd been on the verge of doing the job himself.

By then Warren was thirteen and had all but moved in with Dasie's family. He spent four out of five nights on the dining room sofa or stretched out in a sleeping bag on the floor of Sam's room. When Betsy married Frank, two years later, there was some conversation about how Warren would likely be spending more time at home now.

Somehow it hadn't worked out that way. Not that there was anything wrong with Uncle Frank. But it did just seem that whenever he gave advice, Warren headed as fast as he could in the other direction.

The blaming began after Warren quit high school. Hints about what could have been seen and who should have seen it. Hints that Warren had spent too much time at the Jenson house. Hints that Hank shouldn't have let Warren tag along to Early's Saw Shop. *Early's?!* Dasie's father threw up his hands. His own children had tagged along to Early's most of their lives. It hadn't done *them* any harm.

Early's was where loggers gathered at the end of a workday. They leaned on the beds of their pickup trucks and maybe drank a beer or had a chew, and swapped tales. And although Dasie's father had quit logging six years ago—had come in from the woods and taken the job at the mill—he still liked to drop by Early's from time to time. Dasie, for one, loved to go along. She loved the smell of the dirt and the sawdust and the oil, and she loved the stories, even though she disbelieved half of them. Where the harm was, she could not see.

Dasie looked over at Warren now. He had dampened the dishcloth at the hose and was wiping the table. Wiping it harder than it needed, really; it wasn't so very dirty to begin with. She didn't know: if Warren didn't remember his father, was it like he'd never had one?

Sam made himself busy lighting the charcoal, and Dasie took the pruning shears and carefully cut chrysanthemum blooms. She wandered outside the gate and cut a few black-eyed Susans as well. Then she thought if she walked on down the block a ways she might find some wild sweet peas still in bloom.

In truth, she didn't want to go back in the yard just yet. She felt ashamed. Blurting out about Uncle John had made an awkwardness, had disrupted something, and she didn't know how to fix it.

By the time she returned, Dasie was relieved to see her parents in the yard and the mood utterly changed. Her father sat in a lawn chair under the apple tree with his feet propped on the picnic table bench and a can of cold beer in one hand. And her mother bustled back and forth from the kitchen in her ankle-length sundress, bringing plates and condiments and covered dishes.

The grill sizzled while Sam and Warren turned the ribs and slathered on layer upon layer of sauce. Warren had missed the day's work on the landing. "Not that that's much to miss," he told Hank. "I'd rather be falling trees."

"Don't be in too big a hurry," Dasie's father said. "You're learning there on the landing, whether you know it or not. And you'll need every bit of it later on." Warren seemed to hear and not to hear. He turned back to the grill without comment.

It was the time of day when the inside of any Grace Falls house was hotter than the mountain air, and neighbors were out for a stroll. Some hailed Dasie's dad and Warren and leaned on the fence awhile to talk about the fire. Dasie noticed, though, that her dad never really took his eyes from her mother. And he steered the conversation from actual fire fighting to speculation about how much timber might have been lost or saved. Five hundred thousand board feet, maybe a million, had gone up in smoke.

Her mother returned from yet another trip to the kitchen for cold drinks, looked at Warren, and asked, "Did you remember to phone your parents?"

Warren, suddenly shuffling, said, "Uh, no. I forgot."

"Oh, Warren, you need to do that! Please. And do ask them to come down. Tell them we have plenty of food. We'd love to have them."

Warren sighed and went inside. In a couple of minutes he was back. "They can't come," he said. The relief in his voice was unmistakable. "They said to thank you, but they've got other plans."

He might as well have chucked a pebble into a flock of birds—glances flew in all directions, then one by one returned. Aunt Betsy and Uncle Frank were not mentioned again.

Dasie later thought they'd have made it all the way through the evening—through the country-style pork ribs, through the potato salad, through the beans and the squash and the corn on the cob and the green salad and the corn bread—except that Marsha Epp came puffing down the street. She didn't slow down even, which was fine. But she did wave and call out, "Can't stop. Just having my walk. I have to hurry home to see Hank on TV."

"On *TV*?" Anne Jenson was instantly up from the table. But just as quickly Dasie's dad had a hand on her arm.

"Whoa . . . ," he said.

"Oh, Hank, we have to go see! It must be on the news."

"We don't have to do any such thing," he said. "The last thing I want after fighting a fire all day is to go in that hot house and watch it on TV."

"Well, you could stay here then, and the rest of us could go. It can't take but a few minutes."

Dasie, Sam, and Warren exchanged looks, then studied their plates. Dasie was itching to run inside, but she sensed that the first person who moved toward the house would be followed by her mother.

"You'd abandon me in the middle of this wonderful meal for television?" her father said.

Dasie caught Sam rolling his eyes, and Warren whispered, "Dirty pool." But it worked. Dasie's mom stood for a moment more, obviously torn, then sank slowly to her seat.

Dasie's dad squeezed his wife's hand, and nobody spoke for a moment. Then, just as Dasie thought, Whew! her mother said in a low, even tone, "Hank Jenson, I want you to tell me the truth. Were you and Polly really up on top of those log decks today?"

He hesitated. "Just one of them," he said.

"Oh, Hank! I was so frightened."

"I'm sorry, I never meant for that to happen," he said. "The chief promised to keep radio silence. You'd never have known we were up there if that kid from Morgantown hadn't nearly blown us off with his hose."

"Oh, wonderful! I wasn't supposed to know?

26

That was supposed to keep you safe?" She jerked her hand away.

He shook his head. "Now, Anne, I knew what I was doing. You've got to remember, I've walked logs half my life. It's in my blood. My father could *dance* on logs. He was the best pond man this town ever had."

"And he wore caulk boots! What did you have on? Just a pair of rubber boots."

"With good tread."

"And what was *Polly* wearing? You can't tell me she's experienced walking on logs. You both could have been killed!"

"Polly knows how to take care of herself."

"Are you kidding? Polly Ware doesn't know the meaning of fear. And neither do you!"

For a long while Dasie's father said nothing. It was almost as though he'd gone off somewhere, on a visit to some private place only he could see. His silence seemed to spread out from the table to the far reaches of the yard, broken only by the chirp of crickets somewhere near the woodshed.

At last, gently, he spoke. "Yes, I do," he said. "That's why I'm still here."

JOE: *Pat got stung by a bald-headed hornet today. Nailed him good, right between the eyes. Swelled up something mean and was turning colors before we headed in.*

CURLY: *Generally a bald-headed hornet's negotiable, unless you do something plain stupid, like throw a rock at his nest.*

JOE: *And then you're not just dealing with one hothead.*

CURLY: *No, sir. They come cooking past you like bullets, then circle back to hit you from the front. Bald-headed hornets always favor the eyes.*

JOE: *They do that.*

MARV: *Worst I ever got stung was when I felled a Doug fir on top of a nest of yellow jackets. Never saw that nest. Just stepped backward right into it. Were they mad! I had yellow jackets up my pants, down my shirt, just crawling all over me, stinging as they went. I took off running down the hill, peeling clothes so fast. . . . By the time I got to the landing, I was standing there in just my undershorts and boots. Gave the boys a good laugh. To this day I don't know how I did that. Try as I might, I cannot get my pants off without taking off my boots.*

JOE: *Yellow jackets are good for getting in your clothes. That and in your hair.*

CURLY: *That's what I kept trying to tell that logger out of Twin Forks. Samson, we called him. Wouldn't listen. I began to doubt he ever had worked in the woods.*

MARV: *I remember him. Had a ponytail nearly down to his belt.*

CURLY: *And proud he was of that hair, too. Every morning in camp he brushed it out, then tied it up all tidy. Till the day he got mixed up with a swarm of yellow jackets.*

MARV: *That was a sight—him swatting and clawing, trying to get those jackets out of his hair. Finally had to jump in the crick.*

CURLY: *Next morning he had a haircut just like mine.*

JOE: *You got no haircut, Curly. You're plain bald.*

CURLY: *That's what I'm sayin'.*

three

When twilight came to Grace Falls, it came suddenly. The sun hovered for a moment on the horizon, then made a plunge behind the mountains. Dasie thrilled at the first cool breezes brushing along her skin but in a very few minutes was rubbing her bare arms for warmth. Her father made a quick trip inside and returned with a shawl for her mother and an armload of wool shirts from the hooks by the back door.

The picnic table had been cleared of everything except the vase of flowers and an oil lamp, which Sam now lit against the gathering dark. It seemed to Dasie that her family had a hard time giving up on a summer day. She thought of it as inborn, the way some families ran to flat feet or a taste for trout. Hers shared an unwillingness to say, "This day is done."

Warren and Sam leaned backward against the picnic table, their legs stretched full, ankles crossed.

In the failing light Dasie thought they looked like twins. If you just counted size and shape, posture and gesture, they were almost interchangeable. Through the face they were opposites, though. Sam was dark, almost swarthy, with soft brown eyes that held a steady gaze. Warren was as fair as Sam was dark, and his pale blue eyes moved from place to place, urgent, as though on a search.

The two of them had been like that for as long as Dasie could remember, alike but entirely different. And always, always they'd been best friends.

Now, in the shadowy lamplight, Dasie had the sense a mistake had been made. She believed that a stranger, if asked to choose, would pick Warren as most likely to up and leave Grace Falls. Just watching him could make you jumpy, as though he might unexpectedly vanish. But instead, it was Sam who was leaving. In two weeks, less than that, he'd be gone.

There was never a question Sam would go. Her father always said the facts were simple: for a good job, for security, his children would have to leave Grace Falls when they were grown. Grace Falls was a dead end. And Sam never questioned this any more than Dasie would, though he wasn't sure what there was to do outside of Grace Falls.

Finally he settled on the Navy. He'd see some of the world and, while he was at it, figure out the part about what to do. He said this with a smile and shrug—no big deal.

Still, as summer passed, Sam stuck ever closer

to home, like someone whose glue was starting to set. Dasie watched him lounging easily against the table, and as she did she wondered if he really minded leaving. Sam kept so much to himself, for all she knew he might be looking forward to it. But he looked so . . . *rooted* there, with the lamplit leaves of the apple tree overhead and a blade of grass between his teeth. It was impossible to picture him anyplace else, much less thousands of miles away.

Now, as he leaned forward to scratch Tattler behind the ears, Sam turned to their mother. "You should tell Warren how you and Dad met. Have you ever heard this story, Warren?"

"No," Warren said quickly. "I'd really like to."

A consolation prize, Dasie thought. That would be just like Sam, to give their mother a chance for a story—a way of making up for keeping things from her about the fire. And he knew she loved to tell this one. If Warren had heard it before (and Dasie was suspicious he had), he never let on.

Her mother's face lit up, and she inched forward in her chair. "It was 1976," she said, "right after my freshman year in college. Four of us from my dorm decided to get together for a camping trip. Our big adventure! And I can't remember who suggested the Grace River Campground—Laine, I think—but I do remember it was about halfway between where Laine and Carole lived in Oregon and where Joanne and I lived in the Bay Area.

"Mind you, my parents thought this was a simply dreadful idea, four girls alone in the woods. It took some doing to wear them down. But they finally agreed when I told them the campground had a host couple staying there."

"Harry and Marsha Ware," Dasie's father said. "Polly's grandparents. They were retired by then, and in the summer they made a little extra money that way. Plus, it gave them a change."

"Well, so Joanne and I drove all this way up from the city. And we had this map. But you know me and maps." She laughed. "Somewhere we made a wrong turn, and pretty soon we're on this road which had petered out into dirt. Nothing but trees in every direction. I never saw so many trees! And no sign of the campground. No sign of anything. No *signs,* unless you count those itty-bitty numbered tags they stick on the occasional tree. Imagine this for a city person. We were lost in the deep woods."

"You weren't lost," Dasie's father said. "You were just misplaced."

"We were lost! At least as far as I was concerned. And the car was overheating, too. It was mid-July, and it was hot, hot, hot. We decided to just stop and turn off the engine for a while and try to figure out the map. But when we tried to start up the car again, nothing happened. Nothing. That car was dead.

"Next thing you know, here comes a pickup truck with three of the dirtiest, scroungiest-looking men you've ever seen. They're all wearing hard hats. And they stop. Joanne and I just looked at each other. We knew we were in trouble."

Her father was chuckling now. This was his favorite part of the story.

"So two of these guys get out. Well, let me tell you! They were so filthy. You could just maybe see their eyes and a little skin where sweat ran down and left streaks. I was sure they hadn't bathed in weeks. They were wearing these big heavy boots, and their clothes were black with grime and in *tatters*. All of them!"

Her father laughed. "I think it was the cutoff pant hems that really did her in," he said. "She'd never seen a logger before, so she didn't know we did that on purpose."

Warren threw his head back, joining in the laughter. "Oh, right! And don't forget the cutoff sleeves on the hickory shirts. They fray when you wash 'em, and *then* they'll rip on a limb anyhow."

The color rose in Anne Jenson's cheeks. "Of course it makes perfect sense now. A hem could hang up on a branch. That could mean your life when you're running from a falling tree. But how was I to know?"

"Rags," Dasie's father said. "She thought we were dressed in rags!" He hooted.

"So then the one who'd been driving—"

"That was me. It was my truck. And brand-new, too! Not that she noticed."

"He says, all polite as could be, 'Do you ladies need any help?' Joanne gives me this look again. I think we were both pretty scared. But stranded out there that way, well, we didn't really have a whole lot of choices. So I say, 'Yes, we're having some car trouble.'

"Well, he opens up the hood and tinkers around some and, in about five minutes, has it running again."

"Vapor lock," Dasie's father said. "Not too hard to figure that one."

"Not hard for you maybe! But I was a city person, remember. If your car breaks down, you call a tow truck.

"Anyhow, the car is now running, and the next thing he asks is if we might by any chance be lost. That's how he says it—'by any chance'—and he's just grinning at us. Because of course we are on a logging road which is headed directly *nowhere,* as he perfectly well knows."

"Just being polite," Dasie's father said with a twinkle.

"Joanne throws up her hands and admits we're lost, says we'd appreciate it if they could direct us to the Grace River Campground. And finally *this* one"—she gestured toward Dasie's dad with her thumb—"he says, 'How's about we just *escort* you there, ma'am?'"

"Escort, huh?" Sam said. "Pretty fancy, Dad."

He shrugged. "You do what you can."

"You shush!" Dasie's mom said. "So now we have an escort. And we must have been all of a mile away from the campground the whole time. Really, we were right on top of it. If it'd been a snake, it would have riz up and bit us. In absolutely no time we're there.

"Now, I am very relieved. And grateful, really. Joanne, too. But then I notice that these guys are not turning around and going away as you'd expect. No. They're leading us all the way into the campground and right up to the door of the little trailer that says CAMPGROUND HOST.

"Of course I've figured out by now they're not dangerous criminals or anything, but they're so . . . *uncivilized.* I can just imagine the kind of impression this will make, us arriving in the company of these dirty, raggedy young men. And I no sooner think this than our escort here leans on his horn—really leans on it, a couple of good long blasts—and I about faint with embarrassment.

"The trailer door bursts open and out comes this very nice-looking elderly couple. Terribly clean and presentable, mind you. And the gentleman says to our escort, almost shouting really, 'What seems to be your problem, boy?' "

At this Dasie, Sam, and Warren all burst out laughing. The idea of anyone calling Hank Jenson "boy"!

"And this filthy, disreputable person steps out of the pickup and says, all disgusted like, 'You running a campground here or what? Here I bring you some customers, and you can't even come out to greet 'em! What kind of a host are you, anyway?'

"By now I could simply die of mortification. I

step out of the car, all set to apologize, to try and explain this terribly rude behavior somehow, when all of a sudden they're shaking hands and laughing and hugging and slapping each other on the back! I mean, this campground host and his wife are treating this *ruffian* like he's their long-lost son or something."

"Harry and Marsha always were partial to me," Dasie's dad said.

"Partial! Partial doesn't cover it. Joanne and I might as well have been flyspeck. I mean, we're standing there invisible while this nice old couple, who have clearly lost their minds, are falling all over this dirt god! I could not believe it."

"So how did you get together?" Warren asked, laughing. "I mean, so far this does *not* sound like a love connection."

"Oh, it wasn't!" Dasie's mom said.

"Speak for yourself," said her father. "Harry and Marsha knew. They could see I was eyeing this one, so as I was leaving, they said why didn't I come on out and visit them some evening."

"Which I never even heard," she said. "Or if I did, I certainly didn't think it had anything to do with me."

"And of course I did drive out for a visit with Harry and Marsha. The very next night."

"By which time I'd forgotten all about him. The four of us girls were just lounging around the campfire, roasting marshmallows or something, and no doubt doing a lot of giggling, when along the road come Mr. and Mrs. Ware on their evening rounds. And with them is this guy, this *hunk*. I mean, he was so handsome. And all decked out, but casual, you know? Wearing this western shirt and boots with just the right amount of shine."

"You get that by rubbing the toe of your boot on the back of the opposite leg," Sam said. "Dad taught me that."

"She didn't even recognize me," his father said.

"Well, no! Not at first anyhow. How could I? But when I did, I could hardly believe it was the same person.

"So we all just stand around and visit for a while, and I'm partly embarrassed because of the things I thought the day before. And at the same time I'm trying to figure out whether there's any way I can get to know Hank better, because he's so nice, you know."

"And handsome," Sam said with a twinkle. "Personally, I think it sounds like it was the handsome part that did the trick."

"Well, no, not really. Or it wasn't *just* that."

Everyone laughed, and Dasie's mother covered her face with her hands. "Oh, for heaven's sake! Really, he was very nice! He had very nice manners, honestly."

This was greeted with guffaws, and Sam slapped his thigh. When they'd settled down again, she continued. "Anyway, before they left, Hank asked me, right in front of everyone, would I like to go into Morgantown the next night, 'cause there was this dance." She shook her head. "I don't know. Joanne and the others thought I was crazy. I mean, I was a city girl, a college student with a presumably brilliant future at something. What was I going to do with this . . . *cowboy,* or whatever he was? I didn't even understand then that he was a timber faller.

"Not that it would have made any difference, because I never even thought twice. I just accepted his invitation—quick!—before he took it back."

"And the rest is history," Hank Jenson said.

"Or almost history. We went dancing in Morgantown the next night and the night after that. And Hank was such a gentleman. He never really held my hand until the second night, then just gave me a little peck on the cheek when we said good-bye."

"And got her address," he said with a wry grin. "It was all part of a plan."

"What plan? You got my address, but you never wrote!"

"That was in the plan, too."

"Dad's not much for writing," Dasie said, feeling a sudden need to explain this courtship lapse of her father's.

"The whole winter of my sophomore year I couldn't stop thinking about him. It was awful. I think I was actually lovesick. And I did date some other guys—you know, some nice clean college boys? But I just was not interested.

"So when Hank finally telephoned me, along about May when I believe I had truly given up, and invited me to come up after school was out and stay for a week with his family . . . Well, that was the second time I never even thought twice.

"My parents about had a fit, of course. They had all these plans for me, and none of them included my running off with some logger. Which was how they saw it. And really, they never got over it."

"In a way you'd have to admit they were right," Dasie's father said, "because she never went back. Not for long anyway."

"Just long enough to pack. I stayed with your Grandma and Grandpa Jenson that whole summer. Hank was working in the woods, and I got a job waiting table over in Morgantown. And we saved our money, and in the fall we were married."

"And *now* the rest is history," Dasie's father said, getting to his feet. "And it's also time for bed for old folks." They made the rounds, saying goodnight. Dasie's mom bestowed kisses on everyone. Her dad folded Dasie in a bear hug, then turned to Sam and Warren and solemnly shook hands with each. "You boys did good work today," he said. "I'm proud of you." Sam and Warren both shuffled, embarrassed. But more than that, Dasie knew, they were pleased. There were few things they valued more than her father's praise.

At the foot of the steps he turned back toward Warren. "Soon as you're ready to call it a night, you might head on home," he said. "Your folks would probably appreciate seeing a little something of you."

"Yes, sir," Warren said. "I'll do that."

Sam walked to the table and blew out the oil lamp. In the yard and far beyond, hundreds of crickets sang at top voice, and overhead the August night blazed with a million stars. All at once Dasie was trembling with cold. Only then did it hit her how tired she was. And how very long it had been since the day began.

"I'm going in, too," she said.

Sam wrapped his arms around her. "You're shaking," he said.

"Cold. Even my knees are knocking."

"You'd better go to bed then."

"That's where I'm going," Dasie said. "Night, Sam."

"Good-night. And thanks for holding the fort today, okay?"

"You're welcome. I don't think I was much help, though."

"You were. More than you know."

Dasie turned to say good-night to Warren, but he was gazing off in the direction of the back porch.

"Warren?" she said.

He seemed not to hear her. For a few moments more he stood there, lost in his own thoughts. Then he said, "That's what *I* want. If they ever let me off the landing and let me cut real timber, I want that life. I'll be a timber faller and work in the woods until I'm an old man. And who knows, maybe along the way I'll meet a pretty woman. We'll settle down and have a family, and in the summer we'll cook out in the yard."

It was quiet for a time as they all thought about this. It did sound nice, the way Warren spun it out all simple and easy.

But then Sam shook his head and gave a rueful chuckle. "Do yourself a favor, though," he said. "Try to find a woman more along the lines of Polly Ware. I mean, Mom is great, but at least Polly knows how to read a section marker. *And* she can fix her own car."

DAVE: *Met a youngster the other day claims he made twenty-six thousand dollars cutting last year.*

CLAUDE: *Not around here, he didn't. I been falling thirty years now, never made that much in my life.*

DAVE: *Didn't want to call him a liar. Just asked him how he did that. Claims he only cut big timber.*

BILLY: *Must be doing all his cutting in bars. There's more trees cut in a bar than there ever was in the woods. Big ones, too.*

DAVE: *Biggest tree I ever felled was eight feet, six inches on the stump. Took half a day to get it on the ground.*

PAT: *Time was that wasn't unusual. Now there's few timber fallers left even know how to get a tree that size on the ground without breaking it up in the process.*

BILLY: *This new fella, Floyd, on our crew probably never saw a tree that big.*

CLAUDE: *Kid couldn't lay a tree across a barn if it was leaning on it when he started.*

BILLY: *Thinks when Claude lays six trees out in a nice row it's some kinda accident.*

CLAUDE: *I don't know where he worked before,*

*but this kid don't even use a Humboldt
undercut.*

DAVE: *What is he using?*

CLAUDE: *We call it the Himalayan undercut.
'Cause when he's done, there's trees layin'
every which way. Him-a-layin' here, him-
a-layin' there . . .*

four

It was exactly thirteen days and two hours later that Sam knelt in the dark by the back gate, whispered in Tattler's ear, and ruffled him firmly about the head and neck. He carried his small duffel to the trunk of his mother's car and tossed it in, then turned back toward the house, where a light burned over the back porch. For a long moment he stood quietly, a questioning look in his eyes.

Dasie suddenly wanted to holler, "Stop!" She wasn't ready, nowhere near. Sure, there'd been signs, preparations, people who stopped by to say good-bye and wish Sam luck. But in another way the last two weeks had been so ordinary that she'd been tricked by time. And now it had slithered away.

She wanted to take back the afternoons spent with Monica, the mornings baby-sitting for the Raines children, the bike rides to the Grace Falls swimming hole—all the hours when she hadn't really noticed that Sam was leaving.

Warren had noticed, Dasie was now certain of that. He'd come by each day after work and stayed until well past dark. Weekends he simply stayed. He slept on the sofa in the dining room, and in the mornings Dasie found him there, curled in a ball under the afghan. One evening he and Sam headed off down First Street together in deep conversation and returned hours later without explanation.

Most mornings Sam left the house early with Tattler and his fishing pole and stayed gone till lunch. Afternoons he spent over and under his truck. He repaired the taillight, changed the oil, replaced spark plugs and the fan belt, and then washed and waxed every inch. He scrubbed the floor mats and sprayed all the vinyl with something that made it shine.

Always they ate dinner at the picnic table. Grandma Jenson joined them one evening and told stories about the old days when "Mother Grace," the original lumber company, owned the town and everything in it. Dasie had heard most of the stories dozens of times.

"Imagine," Grandma Jenson said, "if you wanted new wallpaper in the kitchen, you just called Mother Grace, and in a week or so some fellows from the town crew showed up and it was done.

"When Hank was born, we got too crowded, so we phoned the company, and they built us an extra room. Built it up at the mill, then loaded it on a flatbed truck, hauled it down here, and set it in place. Just like that. Mother Grace took real good care of us." Every story ended the same—Grandma Jenson sighed and said, "We'll never see those days again."

As she left, she pressed a silver dollar into Sam's hand, an old one dated 1886. "Your grandpa kept this in his wallet every day of his adult life. He'd want you to have it now."

Monday evening Amy Ware came by. She sat between Sam and Warren on the picnic table bench and talked to Dasie's parents about the paralegal course she'd be taking at Faro Junior College in the fall. Thunderheads gathered, bringing with them the edgy fear of lightning strikes in the woods, and the talk turned to forest fires. Only as Amy left did Dasie realize she had come to say good-bye. Sam held her hand as he walked her to the gate, then, although Dasie knew she shouldn't, she watched as Amy stood on tiptoe to kiss Sam's cheek and threw her arms around him in a tight hug.

Then, Tuesday, Dasie walked into her room and found Sam's blue-and-white football jersey laid out on her bed. GRACE FALLS HIGH SCHOOL, it said. Number 25. She picked it up, walked out through the kitchen and dining room to the hall that led to Sam's room, and knocked on his door.

"Come in," he called.

Nothing could have prepared her for the sight. "It's empty!" she cried. "Sam, where's all your stuff? Where are your *things*?"

"Oh, they're here," he said, "most of them anyway. You just can't see them."

Dasie scanned the room. The walls were bare, Sam's posters and maps nowhere to be seen. The tops of his dresser and desk, always fatally littered with papers, books, rocks, pinecones, trophies, and small mysterious machine parts, were now completely bare. The stacks of magazines and cascading piles of CDs were gone, along with his fishing poles, lures, and random items of clothing that usually hung from the bedposts or doorknobs or lay in heaps on the floor.

"It looks like a motel room," Dasie said. "It's so . . . *vacant.*"

"Cool. That was the idea. Check this out." He opened up four dresser drawers. They were completely empty. "Don't look in the other two," he said. Then he opened the closet door. "Check this," he said. There were five cartons neatly stacked with his name printed in black marker on the sides. His baseball mitt hung from a hook, and his pool cue stood in the back corner.

"I took three bags of junk to the dump. I mean, it finally dawned on me that I'm a pack rat, and maybe I don't need all this stuff. Of course there are a few boxes stuck out in the garage, too, including my world-class collection of Lego. I hate to admit it, but that really hurt, packing up my Lego." He smiled a crooked smile. "Go figure."

"Oh, Sam. You could have just left it. I mean, it's your room." Dasie sat on the edge of his bed, the jersey clutched in her lap.

"Yeah, but that's silly," he said. "This house is

small enough as it is. And I thought you might even want to have this room now. It's bigger than yours, and when I come home on leave, I can stay in the back room just as easily."

So many times over the years Dasie had wished to have Sam's room. Hers was so narrow and cramped. In this room she could spread out, decorate with her own things—it could be the room of her imaginings.

But now, when it was finally offered to her, she looked around and her eyes filled with tears. She shook her head. "I don't think so," she said. "My room's fine, really. And I'm used to it, you know?"

Sam sat beside her and put an arm around her shoulders. "Hey, you're not going to go all gooey on me now, are you?"

"No. Yes. I mean, I think it just now hit me that you're really leaving. But I never thought it would be like this." She hid her face in the jersey, flushed and miserable.

"Hey," Sam said again. "It might take a minute to get used to. But you'll manage. I'm counting on you, Dasie. You've always been the strong one in this family."

"I don't know where you ever got an idea like that," she said. It came out muffled through the jersey.

"Ah, but you are," Sam told her. "I've always known that about you, ever since you were five years old and stomped home mad from the ballpark. Do you remember?"

Dasie shook her head.

"Well, I'll never forget it," Sam said. "Warren and I were playing and Dad was umpire, and you couldn't understand why you were only allowed to watch. You never even said you were leaving. Just marched off, and nobody noticed."

"Oh, no," Dasie said. It was starting to sound familiar, like something she'd do if she was really mad.

Sam went on. "And when you got home, as if it wasn't bad enough you were alone, you told Mom you'd been chased by a bear. In broad daylight. Down Old Mill Road!"

Dasie groaned. "I remember that. The thing is, I got scared about halfway home, and I was afraid something would get me. I ran the rest of the way and actually believed I'd been chased. I'm not sure I knew I was telling a lie."

"Well, you convinced Mom. That's what amazes me. Like you'd still be here if a bear had decided to chase you? She was fit to be tied when we got in. *Mad?* She came this close to throwing things at all of us, Dad included."

Dasie was suddenly regretful. "Some brat, huh?" she said.

"Maybe, maybe not," Sam said. "But I'll say this—I never really worried about you after that. I thought, Here's a kid who can look out for herself." He laughed and gave an easy sideways shove to her head.

Dasie smiled a little and rubbed at her nose with

the jersey. "I guess I've always had this feeling I *could* look after myself, even though I've never had to," she admitted. "I mean, I've always had you and Warren."

"You see?" Sam said. "And you know Mom and Dad—sometimes they need looking out for themselves. Mom especially. She needs someone to haul her back when she goes over, the deep end about something."

Dasie nodded.

"And keep a grip on Dad, too," Sam went on. "I mean, in a couple of more years you'll be headed to high school, and boys will be following you home. It's my prediction he's going to try to lock you in a tower when that happens."

Dasie smiled in spite of herself. "If you knew the boys in my class, you wouldn't say that. They're all geeks."

"Oh, I know them, all right," Sam said. "One or two will shape up okay. You'll see. Of course, all the girls in my class thought the same about me, so who am I to say?"

"You turned out okay," Dasie said. "You turned out fine!"

"Ah!" Sam said, standing. "I guess this means you'll be wanting to keep that football jersey?"

"Can I?" Dasie asked. "Really?"

"It's yours. But I do want to point out that it did not have snot on it when I gave it to you."

Dasie laughed and snapped it at him. "Butthead," she said. She stood and walked to the window. Sam's room looked out on the vegetable garden and woodshed. It struck her as a very Sam-ish view—it had been his chore for years to carry in the firewood, and he'd put the chicken wire around the vegetable garden himself. Soon in the mornings he'd wake up and look out on . . . who knew what?

"Do you think you'll like the Navy?" she asked.

Sam sighed and joined her at the window. "I don't know," he said. "I mean, honestly, Dasie, you're supposed to know what you want to do with your life by the time you graduate high school, and I don't have a clue. Not one."

"Well, that's the same with me," Dasie said. "I think of things once in a while, like I'll be a famous actress or something and make tons of money. But in the other part of my mind I know that's dumb."

"Yeah, but you have plenty of time yet. Me . . . Well, I sorta ran out of time. But the Navy has a lot of things you can get training in. Maybe I'll stumble across something I like."

"You will. I mean, most likely."

"I hope so," Sam said. Then he laughed. "Any-how, I look at it this way—the Navy's going to own me for a few years. At least that'll keep me from running back home."

Dasie turned sharply around. "Do you think you'd do that," she asked, "run back home?"

"I might. Who knows?" He shrugged. "I've never really been anyplace but here. Oh, sure, we've been to see Grandma and Grandpa Tolbert in San

Francisco, and I went to Oregon to ski a couple of times. But unless you count away games in high school, that's about it. I don't know how I'll like it someplace else."

Dasie understood what he meant. Sometimes when she watched TV, she'd see places that looked beautiful or exciting and think it would be fun to live there. But then when she watched the news, all those same places seemed pretty scary.

"If you want to know the truth," Sam said, "that's why I'm taking the train. I need to leave slowly. I figure it should be gradual, so I can get used to it as I go along." He paused, then turned away and added, "And also so I can be sure it's real."

The next day Sam taped a FOR SALE sign in the window of his pickup. He spent the better part of that morning replacing the torn back-door screen to exclamations of delight from their mother. Then in the afternoon he mowed the lawn and ran the Weed Eater, then set the sprinklers out. He leaned against the fence and surveyed the scene with a look that Dasie had sometimes seen on her father's face— a look of enormous satisfaction, as though what he rested his eyes on was the most prideworthy thing in all the world.

Suddenly, as if gripped by a mania, Sam ran inside for the camera and started taking pictures of everything in sight. First a photo of his truck, then of the house and yard from three different angles; then he asked Dasie to pose with Tattler. Next he called to their mother, who fussed with her hair and lipstick before she'd let him point the camera her way.

Late in the afternoon Grandma Jenson stopped by with a peach pie, and by then Warren was home from the woods and Hank from the mill, so the camera came out again. Everyone posed in every conceivable combination until along about the middle of the second roll some of them started mugging, and Sam said, "That's it. I don't want to remember my family as a bunch of goons."

After dinner, Sam, Warren, and Dasie piled into Sam's pickup, Dasie in the middle, and drove up to the mill, where Sam took more pictures. Then in the fading light they cruised town, snapping pictures at the high school, the baseball park, and even out at the dump, where three large cinnamon bears were "immortalized," as Warren said, in the middle of their evening meal.

In front of the post office the second roll ran out. Sam rewound the film and placed it firmly in Dasie's hand. "Get this developed as soon as my truck is sold and send the prints to me. Warren will give you the money. But don't leave it up to him—he'll never get it done."

"Hey!" Warren said. "When did I ever let you down?"

"Never," Sam said. "But when was the last time you went to Morgantown?"

"Well . . . not lately."

"See? Warren never goes to Morgantown. He

never leaves Grace Falls if he can help it. Except to go to the woods. Don't start thinking he'll drive to Morgantown for a lousy roll of film."

"Well, I *would*. . . ."

"Never mind," Dasie said. "I can do it. I'm going over with Monica on Saturday anyway. We're getting some home perms so we can do our hair before school starts."

"Oh, no!" Warren said. "Say it ain't so, Dasie. Am I going to have to disown you?"

"Sounds like I'm leaving Grace Falls just in time." Sam laughed.

"You are both such big jerks." Dasie tossed her head. "You're going to be so sorry someday when I look incredibly fabulous and I get married to an awesome prince and I don't invite *either* of you to my wedding!"

"Oh, no you don't," Sam said. "I'll be there. I don't care if you get married on Mars. I'll be there."

"We'll both be there," Warren said. "It's my lasting ambition to dance with you at your wedding, Miss Dasie-Mae, and I'll be there even if I have to fight my way in."

For a moment Dasie felt weakened, dazed by the love of these two. When had they ever *not* been there for her? She was swamped with memories of squirt-gun fights, toboggan rides, careening down the street behind one or the other of them on a bicycle seat. When Jessie Baxter punched her in the eye over some third-grade wrong, they both showed up at the end of school, menacing, "We're her bodyguards, see?" Only Dasie knew neither of them would hurt a fly.

"You big, hairy clowns," she said. And then, afraid she might disgrace herself with tears, she drew herself up and said, "Fine, but I just want to remind you of one thing."

"What's that?" Sam said.

"Look around this truck and tell me, who's the real cowboy?"

"The one in the middle!" they both howled.

"And don't you forget it!" she said.

Now, in the backseat of their mother's car, Dasie wished more than anything to have the last weeks back again, to notice every minute as she hadn't the first time. At last Sam climbed into the seat beside her, and as they left for the train station in Faro, he did not look back.

Hank drove slowly over the mountain pass, wary of the sudden appearance of migrating deer. The trees beside the road reached upward, beyond the headlights of the car, to meet, Dasie imagined, in a peak somewhere in the dark. Too soon, they reached Morgantown, then the freeway, and too soon again Faro and the station.

The station was deserted save for the manager, who occasionally crossed the tracks with a light in hand. Sam, it seemed, would be the only passenger at this stop. And the train, as ever, was late.

The wait in the dark was agonizing. Dasie wished the train would hurry up and get there, and she wished it would never come. Every few minutes her mother spoke.

"You know, you can always call us collect. From anywhere. Anytime. It doesn't matter."

"Yeah, I know, Mom. Don't worry," Sam said.

Then later, "Now, if you get sick, be sure to let someone know. I mean, you can't expect people who don't know you to just guess."

"I know, Mom. I'll be okay. Promise."

The minutes in between were heavy with silence. Dasie's father paced, stopping now and again to set his hand silently on Sam's shoulder. Then, suddenly—almost without warning, as though it was the very last thing any of them expected—there came a whistle and a light from the bend, and the train was upon them. It stood massive and gleaming on the track, heaving as though alive. After all the waiting there was now a rush, a blur. Hugs that were too short and a jumble of good-byes. And then the doors slid closed, and the train moved out with an astonishing silky glide and was gone in the night.

Dasie's parents leaned into each other and stared down the empty track. Dasie stood with her arms wrapped around her chest, her cheeks wet, and heard the echo of her brother's voice: "I need to leave slowly . . . so I can be sure it's real."

five

It took more than a minute to get used to having Sam gone. Much more. Sometimes the better part of a day passed when Dasie didn't think of him, but each time she did, she remembered how very far away he was. It was a distance that could be *felt*. And he'd left so little behind, such small traces. She opened the door to his room just once and closed it again. It was awful what he'd done to his room. But the most startling thing was how she missed him, unexpectedly, in doorways, in the vast space made by his absence.

Tattler moped. He slept outside the door to Sam's room and in the mornings sat woefully at the back gate, as though he'd been left behind from a fishing trip.

Dasie's mother took it quietly. But it was a brooding kind of quiet. She hovered near the phone at first, until Sam called to say he'd arrived. Then, with nothing further to do for him, she grew restless, distracted. Sometimes she wandered out to the back porch and gazed off at the rolling horizon to the south, and after a bit heaved a sigh, then came back in. Other times she folded an item of laundry, then turned right around and folded it again. Her brow seemed perpetually furrowed in concentration. Dasie was wary of speaking to her, afraid of interrupting. She felt helpless to do anything but watch as each day her mother grew more . . . *taut.*

Also, there was the near total absence of Warren. Dasie had somehow not counted on this. She doubted her mom had either. As she thought about it, Dasie reminded herself that, after all, it was Sam he'd come to see; there was hardly a reason for him to stop by now. Yet somehow Warren's absence made Sam's echo all the louder, and Dasie thought it made them all edgy.

It may have been miscalculation, or maybe it was inevitable, but on Sunday morning, as Dasie shook the orange juice and her mother beat eggs in a bowl, her father said mildly, "What's going on, Anne? You're wound up tighter than a ten-day clock."

With that Dasie's mother slammed the bowl on the counter and flung the fork in the sink. "With *me?* Our son is out there—God knows where— with a bunch of strangers, and you want to know what's going on with *me?* What I want to know is what's wrong with *us?* How could we let this happen?"

Dasie froze. She hated it when her parents quarreled. It made her feel as though they'd lost their minds, become crazy people. Nothing they argued about ever seemed worth it. And yet she was afraid to leave the room, as if doing so would draw more attention to what was happening. She stood motionless, the orange-juice carton in her hands.

Her father looked dumbfounded. "How could we let *what* happen? Anne, we didn't 'let' anything happen. We planned this," he said.

"Well, it was a terrible mistake," her mother shouted, "a terrible, terrible mistake!"

"No, Anne, what? I don't know what you're thinking. We talked about this for years!"

"No, *you* talked. I agreed. And we were wrong, Hank Jenson. Anything that feels this bad is wrong. It's a mistake!" All at once she was red faced. She snatched up a dish towel and flailed it helplessly in the air, then turned sharply away.

For a minute Dasie's father stood slack jawed, mute. Dasie was afraid he might turn on his heel and stalk off. He could do that, in a heartbeat. But instead he slumped backward against the kitchen counter. "I just don't understand you," he said. "There's no future here for Sam. You know that. We want better for him than this."

Dasie's mother turned back to face him. "And what's wrong with this, I'd like to know? This life is good enough for us, isn't it? We're happy, aren't we? So why wasn't it good enough for Sam?"

"Because it's *over*!" he said. "It's been over for

years. We're all on borrowed time here, Anne. You know that."

"I don't know that," she said. "Not anymore. You've been saying that almost since the day we met, but we're still here. *That's* what I know. We're here, and Sam's gone."

Dasie's father shoved his hands in his pockets and paced the kitchen floor. "All right, so tell me, Anne, do you want to talk about this? I mean, what part don't you understand?"

Dasie could see he was starting to fume, and she thought, Uh-oh, here it comes.

"Do you want to talk about armchair conservationists who sit in their wood-frame houses on their beautiful hardwood furniture, drinking wine cured in oak barrels, all the while using several tons of extra paper to persuade the world that *nobody should ever cut another tree*? Do you want to talk about what it takes to keep a small mill like ours running when labor and logs are cheaper in other parts of the world? Do you want to talk about how our lives depend on decisions made by politicians and judges who have no idea how to grow a tree, far less run an ecological, sustainable-yield timber operation?" His voice rose steadily as he spoke. "I mean, what part do you want to talk about? *Is there something going on here you don't understand?*"

Dasie was paralyzed. She'd heard it all before, of course—many times and in several versions. And not just from her father. Down at Early's or the market or even on a street corner, everyone talked the same. But her father had never railed at her mother about it before.

Dasie's mom groped toward a chair and collapsed into it. "None of it," she said. "I don't want to talk about any of it, Hank. I'm sick of talking. I only know that our boy is gone and that we sent him away. And he's so young. He's *so* young, and he's so far from home."

Dasie's father sighed. He moved forward, wrapped his arms around his wife's shoulders, and laid his head on her neck. "Anne, I know it's hard," he said.

"Hard? Oh, Hank, it's worse than hard. I feel like somebody ripped my heart right out." She dissolved in tears, in big heaving sobs, while Dasie's dad held her and stroked her head.

In time she slowly wound down, and Dasie felt a creeping relief. The worst, she felt, was now past. Her mother would go on missing Sam, like she did, like her father did. But not so terribly now. Not quite so hard.

School started the following Tuesday. If anyone had told Dasie a month ago that she'd be glad to go back, she'd have called them foolish or worse. She'd dreaded it, really—the same eighteen kids she'd known since kindergarten, and this year the unlovable and unloved Mrs. Gower, known for strict rules and lots of homework.

Dasie went off the first day with a short new

haircut, paid for from her baby-sitting money and meant to disguise the perm, which had been a disaster. She was glad Sam was not there the day she'd come home from Monica's with her hair more bent than curled in some places and flat in others. Now she thought she more resembled a rag doll than anything else. But she wore Sam's jersey, and some blush that her mother said she didn't need, and Monica declared she was going down to Lila's Locks the very next day to have her hair cut the same.

Mrs. Gower waited until the second day to assign homework, but by then Dasie'd made up her mind that this would be the year she reformed. She'd go straight home and do her homework first thing. Which she did for the first week.

Saturday, Warren sold Sam's truck to a kid from Morgantown. Dasie was glad it was going out of town. It would be too weird to see someone driving around town every day in Sam's truck. Warren handed her mother a little over six hundred dollars in cash, saying Sam wanted it put in his savings account, except for the money owed Dasie for photographs. Then for a while he and Dasie's dad were out by the woodshed, tinkering earnestly with their saws.

Later Dasie's dad came in the house and said, "I've set it with Warren to go woodcutting in the morning. I think we'd be smart to get one more load for the winter."

Dasie and her mother looked at each other and burst out laughing. Every year it was the same. Their woodshed was full by late June, yet Hank always itched for one more load. This was his third "one more load" of the year.

"Expecting an early winter, are we?" Dasie's mom asked.

"Well, you never can tell."

"He misses his saw," Dasie said.

"Well, now, it's a fact I do miss my saw," he protested, "but if the almanac is right, we could have snow by the first week in November. Anyhow, Warren thinks Betsy and Frank could use another load, too."

"Oh, I'm sure they could," Dasie's mom said, "and your mother, too, no doubt!" Grandma Jenson used kerosene heat, not wood.

Nevertheless, they were all up before daybreak the next morning. They dressed in their oldest clothes—jeans, layers of shirts, and work boots or sturdy shoes. Dasie helped her mother pack the cooler with deviled eggs, cold chicken, sliced tomatoes and cucumber, fruit, and plenty of cold drinks. They stuffed work gloves in their pockets, and Dasie's dad loaded the cooler and his saw in the pickup just as Warren's headlights swept the corner.

Dasie rode in the cab of Warren's truck along with Tattler. It would be a long drive in the dawning light, more than thirty miles along winding road to the better areas of those allowed on the checkerboard Forest Service map. Both trucks had CBs, and Warren stayed about a quarter mile behind Dasie's parents. From time to time Hank's voice came over: "Range cattle up here on the left," or "Camper truck headed your way. Watch him—he's taking the curves a little wide."

As they gained elevation, Dasie saw patches of frost along the road. She thought maybe the almanac would be right this year.

Warren asked about school, so she told him about her resolve to turn over a new leaf. "Good for you," he said. "Mrs. Gower will like you better than she did me. I was not her favorite Jenson." He grinned. "But of course I didn't make things real easy on her. That was the year I decided I hated school."

"Because of Mrs. Gower?" Dasie asked. It was possible. Even Dasie, who liked most people, was having trouble finding a way to like Mrs. Gower.

"Not really. Not that she helped. But I had a couple of teachers in high school I liked even less."

"I think I can guess who they were," Dasie said. "Sam had a few things to say. . . ."

Just then Dasie's dad came over the CB again. "Warren, you're going to see my rig pulled off to the right up here. I could use a hand if you don't mind."

Warren picked up the handset. "Sure thing," he said.

When they came upon her parents' truck, Warren set his hazard lights and then stepped out to join her father in the road. That's when Dasie saw it—a dead fawn on the asphalt. She hid her face in her hands for several minutes until Warren climbed back in. When she looked again, it was gone.

"I hate that," Dasie said.

"Yeah," Warren said. "Me, too." His voice was thick. After a moment he said, "That fawn was fresh killed. What frosts me is the son of a bitch who hit it didn't even stop to get it out of the road. Your dad spotted the mama doe standing off to the side in the trees."

"Oh! That's so sad."

"It's worse than sad," Warren said. "Any minute that doe would've been standing over her dead baby. She'd have stood there all day. Pretty soon we'd have had two dead deer instead of one." He shook his head. "I don't understand some people."

Dasie didn't either. She'd always been taught to be careful of life. All life. Her father even honked at chipmunks to chase them from the roadway. Any drive during chipmunk breeding season was a constant *toot, toot, toot*ing down the road.

The ride was quiet for the next several miles. Then they took a turn and left the pavement. Through several more forks and bends they traveled dirt roads and abandoned logging trails, past trees that grew dense in some places and thin in others. Finally, just beyond an area of plantation, they turned into a stand of trees that mostly looked to be dead and dying. There they stopped.

Dasie remembered with a rush how much she loved this. The sun just barely glanced along the tops of the tallest trees, and the cold air was full of the light scent of pine and fir. And dirt. It was the smell of the earth she loved most, the way it wafted up through the broken frost as they walked around the trucks.

She joined her mother leaning against the warm hood of her father's pickup as he and Warren went off together in search of snags. Tattler meandered along with them, alternately sniffing and prancing. For a long time they were in view, walking side by side, stopping now and then to look up, point, then look and point again. Dasie wasn't sure exactly how this part worked. She only knew they were deciding which snags they'd cut and in which direction they'd lie.

Her mother sighed. "Times like these, he reminds me so of his father," she said.

"Dad?" Dasie asked. She'd never thought of her father as being especially like Grandpa, though she supposed he might be.

"No, Warren," her mother said. "Just looking at him there, walking side by side through the woods that way with your father. It's almost like John is here again." She pressed a hand to her cheek and sighed again. "I saw them like that so often. They were such good friends."

Of course. Her dad and Uncle John *would* have cut firewood together. After all, they'd logged together. Dasie couldn't say why she'd never thought of it.

Then she had another thought. Her mouth

turned dry, but she had to ask. "Mom, was Dad with Uncle John when he was killed?"

"No. Yes. Not really." She turned and faced Dasie. "Your father was nearby, but not right there, Dasie. He was on the same crew, but that day he was jacking a tree farther along. John didn't jack trees. He climbed them instead."

"Oh," Dasie said. She knew some trees had to be climbed before they could be felled. To take the top out. Climbing was one of the most dangerous jobs of all. "Is that what happened? He was climbing?"

"No. No, it was just dumb, really. One of those senseless things. His partner was falling a tree, and he didn't realize John was so close. And John was maybe not paying attention for a minute. But the tree took a turn—who knows why—just far enough for a limb to clip John. Just a little limb, no more than four inches across. But even a small limb from that height lands with such tremendous force, Dasie. The only blessing is John probably never knew what hit him."

Dasie was silent for several minutes. It was all too easy to imagine, with her father and Warren now out of sight. For the first time ever, she had a chill of apprehension about her father. And about Warren. She huddled deeper inside her flannel shirt.

Then she recollected the original intent of her question. "Did Dad *see* it?" she asked.

"No!" her mother said. "Oh, thank God, no. He was about three hundred yards away. Someone came running for him, of course, but there was nothing to be done." A distant look settled on her as she continued. "But I think your dad felt he should have been there. Like maybe he could have stopped it? Or even . . . even that it should have been him. After all, John was the older, the more experienced faller."

For the rest of the morning Dasie lurched between the present and a past—a past that was over before she ever drew breath. For the first time her uncle John seemed real to her.

Her father and Warren returned for their saws, then went off again, Tattler on their heels. In a few minutes she heard the buzz of the saws, then a faint "H'up! H'up!" and a snag hit the ground with a roar like distant thunder. Always before, to hear a tree fall, to see the dust rise and the snag lying neatly exactly where it was intended had made her want to applaud. Now she felt the possibility of catastrophe.

She watched from closer range as Warren and her father limbed the trees; then she and her mom took their chalks and measuring tapes and marked them for bucking. The mingled odors of oil and sawdust, a smell so deeply thrilling she'd sometimes tagged along to Early's for that alone, were now oddly subdued. Uncle John's ghostly presence was, to Dasie, there with them, muffling joy.

They worked steadily, a practiced team loading the rounds into the trucks. Then her father tacked the permits onto the top round, and her mother unloaded food from the cooler onto the tailgate.

They were dirty and tired and, in the noon sun, hot. But the mood was festive, and Dasie did her best to join in. They'd finished a big job. Two trucks were piled high with wood for the winter, and they'd done it together.

On the way home, Tattler put his head in Dasie's lap and fell asleep. Warren drove silently, casting sideways glances at Dasie. Suddenly he apologized. "I'm sorry I said that about Mrs. Gower, Dasie. I didn't mean to upset you. Really, you're a good enough student that you won't have trouble with her. I just had a bad attitude."

"No!" Dasie said. "I wasn't even thinking about that. You didn't upset me. Really. I'm fine."

"Well, if I didn't upset you, something did. You're not yourself. Was it the fawn?"

"No, it wasn't that. I'm fine, really." And then she said, "It's Sam. I miss him, that's all." As she spoke it felt like the truth.

"Ah," Warren said. He seemed to sag. "I miss him, too, Dasie. It was kinda weird today getting wood without him, huh?"

Dasie drew herself up. "We had a postcard from him yesterday," she said, forcing cheer into her voice. "It said, and I quote,

'Dear Mom, Dad, Dasie,
  The air is full of water here. I guess that's why they train the Navy in Chicago so they can learn to inhale water. Today we had haircuts.
  I stood in line for 3 hours just for a haircut

if you can believe that. No leaning on the bulkhead either. Guess they'll get me in shape though.

                         Love, Sam'

"That was it. The whole thing."

Warren slapped the steering wheel. "I don't believe it! The card he sent me said almost exactly the same thing, word for word. What a turkey!"

Dasie laughed now. "Honest?" she said. "Well, I guess that figures. Sam always was kind of sparing with words. Economical, Mom calls it."

"He had his moments, though," Warren said. Then he was almost wistful. "I wonder how he's doing, though. Really."

"I don't know," Dasie said. "We only talked to him just once, and mostly all he said was the trip was okay. No, 'interesting,' I think he said."

"Interesting? Huh. Yeah, I guess it would be." He drove on quietly for a while longer, squinting now and then against the sun. Then he said, "You know, Dasie, I don't think I could do it. I don't believe I could live someplace besides Grace Falls."

"Sure you could," Dasie said. "Dad always says we're all stronger than we think."

"Well, maybe your family's stronger than mine."

"It's the same family, Warren! We're all Jensons, remember?"

"Well . . . suppose I'm the weak link?" he said, with a faintly mischievous twinkle.

Dasie decided he was ribbing her, so she said,

"That's not what *I* hear. You're supposed to be the one with the wild hair."

Warren hooted at that. "A wild hair, eh? Is that what they call it? Well, that explains a lot."

Dasie had again the sensation of having gone too far, of having spoken aloud something she should have kept to herself. "Well, I don't think it's meant in a bad way," she said. "I mean, really, we all think you're great. Just different."

Now she'd gone from bad to worse. Dasie groaned. But Warren just laughed again.

"Different. No, it's okay, Dasie, *different*'s fair. I mean, let's face it, what do you say about a kid who quits geography class because the book is five years old and all the countries have changed anyway? *Different* is a nice way of putting it.

"And maybe the wild hair part is true, too. I just have a hard time understanding when people tell me I can't do things I know perfectly well I *can*. You know?"

Dasie nodded. She understood that part. Like when she wanted the training wheels taken off her first bike, and her parents refused until they found her with a wrench trying to do it herself.

"The thing is, Dasie, I always feel like I'm being held back, you know? Ever since I was really little I've known exactly what I wanted to do. And ever since I was really little, someone has been telling me I can't do it, or I'm not ready. But I am ready. I know I am."

Dasie nodded again. But at the same time she

felt she was in way over her head. She'd never had a conversation like this with Warren before, where he'd talked to her as an equal. And now she was pretty sure that was the one thing she wasn't.

They drew up to the intersection of the highway leading back to Grace Falls. Warren took the turn slowly, one eye on the shifting load of wood in the bed of the truck. Then, as they straightened out again, he said, "Can you keep a secret, Dasie? I mean, not long, just for a few days?"

"Sure," Dasie said. "I guess so."

"Cool. 'Cause I want it to be a surprise. I'm changing jobs. I signed on with Johnson Logging. They're going to let me fall timber."

"Oh!" Dasie said. The whole morning came rushing back to her. The *kaaa-boooom!* of the trees meeting the earth. A remembrance, as though she'd been there, of her uncle John on the ground.

"Think of it, Dasie. A real timber faller. After all this time."

CLAUDE: *I'm still waitin' to see if young Donny Shaw's going to make a timber faller. I ain't bettin' on him.*

JOE: *Most injured logger I ever saw in one cutting season. I doubt he's worked two straight weeks for injury.*

PAT: *I never expected to see him back after he got cold-cocked by that sapling and bit his tongue near clean off. But there he came, hauling his self back as soon as he could eat thick soup.*

CLAUDE: *I must have packed him out to the doctor three times myself. I told him, "You get hurt again, I'll kill you myself with a club. I'm gettin' too old to be packing injured loggers out of the brush."*

PAT: *It wasn't a week later he cut his big toe off with a saw.*

CLAUDE: *I saw his boot flappin' open and blood and said, "What'd you do now, Donny?" He says, "It's just a scratch." Drove himself to the doctor that time.*

JOE: *He might make a logger then. That's how you tell anymore—man walks out of the woods alive, he's a logger.*

CLAUDE: *That's a fact.*

six

"Johnson Logging!" her father cried. It was a week later, and Dasie, her parents, and Warren were seated around the kitchen table. Warren had just arrived and was working on the remains of pancakes, of which Dasie's mom had made far too many. She claimed she couldn't get used to cooking for three, as though she'd never before made more than they could eat.

"The guy's a crook, Warren," her father said. "You don't want to be working for Johnson."

"Well, I don't want to be bumping knots on the landing for the rest of my life either," Warren said. "Anyhow, I don't think it's proved he's a crook."

"Hell, if it could be proved, the man would be out of business or in jail. Both! You'd better do some checking, son. Ask around down at Early's. The boys will tell you."

Warren pushed another piece of pancake in his mouth and shrugged. "Okay, I'll ask. But it doesn't really matter. I'm going to work for him anyway. I already gave my notice with Weston."

Dasie saw her parents' eyes meet in quick communication. Her mother quietly rose from the table and began clearing dirty plates. Dasie grabbed her glass of milk and gulped it down, then took it to the sink. She turned the water on to a slow trickle.

"Well, now, that's backward thinking if I ever heard it," her father said. "You really believe you won't care when your paycheck's short?"

"Well, I suppose. Sure. But right now I need experience more than I need money."

"What experience?" Her father's voice brushed close to anger. "That man couldn't break in a cutter if he wanted to. Which he doesn't. All that matters to him is getting trees on the ground, and he doesn't much care how he does it. I don't like this, Warren. Not one bit." He stood and refilled his coffee cup, then set it on the table, turned his chair around backward, and sat again, straddling it.

Warren laid his fork down and pushed his plate away. He ran a hand through his hair and said, "You know, I suppose I didn't expect you to tell me I was ready to start cutting, 'cause you never said that yet. But I guess I came here hoping for some encouragement. I'm *ready* to start falling, Hank. I know I am, even if you and Mom and Frank don't think so."

Dasie stiffened. It wasn't often her father got lumped in with Aunt Betsy and Uncle Frank.

"Look," her father said, "I know Johnson from the old days. He worked for Mother Grace when I did. And let me tell you, son, there's timber fallers and there's butchers. Johnson's a butcher." He picked up a spoon and stirred his coffee, even though he drank it black. Then he went on. "Warren, I can't stop you from doing this if your mind's made up. Nobody can. But I'm going to tell you something. The first chain saw you ever held in your hands was mine, and I was standing right beside you with my hands next to yours. Remember?"

Warren nodded, his eyes fixed on the table in front of him.

"Well, so if you do this, you're going to learn to be a timber faller. A good one. Not a butcher. 'Cause I'm telling you now, if you're anything less than a first-class faller, I'm going to take it personally."

Warren's head snapped up and he met the steely gaze of Dasie's father, and for a moment Dasie had the sensation he was about to bolt. Then he straightened up some in his chair and said, quietly, "Yes, sir, I understand."

It seemed as though neither of them moved for quite a while. Finally Warren said, "I know Weston's a better outfit than Johnson. You're right. But I'll never get a chance there, that's the trouble. They got all the best fallers in the business, and not one of them has said a word about retiring."

Her father was quiet a moment, then asked, "So what are you going to do?"

"I don't know exactly. I'll watch, I guess. Pay attention. Try to learn the right way from the wrong way." He was floundering, and all at once Dasie felt sorry for him. Her father still had him locked in his piercing gaze.

"No." Hank Jenson shook his head. "You're going to do more than that, Warren. You're going to listen to *me*. You're going to come by in the evenings and tell me where you're cutting and what you're cutting. You'll walk me through what you've done. And when you have a hazard tree, one that you know could kill you and you don't know how to get it on the ground, you're going to walk away from it, you hear? You'll leave it and come here, and we'll talk it down together. And then you'll go back the following day and cut it. Understand?"

Warren, wide eyed, nodded again.

Hank's gaze never wavered, and after another moment of silence he laid the coffee spoon on the table and slid his hand out to Warren. "If this is our deal, I mean us to shake on it," he said.

Dasie was afraid Warren might refuse, and then she saw he was only surprised. He shot his hand out and grabbed Hank's. The shake was firm, emphatic, and as it ended a smile crept over Warren's face.

Dasie's dad stood and clapped Warren across the shoulder. "Come on now," he said. "I need some help sorting out that woodshed. Somehow I've got more wood than I got space."

Dasie dried the dishes while her mother washed, listening all the while to a steady *thock, thock, thock* from the woodshed. When the kitchen was clean, she rushed out to join in the stacking, handing off to Warren as the last row was laid in place. The woodshed was full to groaning, stacked seven feet high and three rows deep on either side. Only a narrow passage remained down the middle. Her father raked up stray chips, then, sizing up the job, nodded. "That should do 'er. Let the snow begin."

Dasie laughed. It was the same every year. When her father said, "Let the snow begin," he meant he was putting up his saw until spring.

Dasie's mother came down the back steps with cotton gloves in one hand and pruning shears in the other. "Did I hear someone say *snow*? Bite your tongue, Hank Jenson. I've still got tomatoes on the vine, not to mention some other work to do around here. Indian summer has only started."

Warren reached in his back pocket and pulled out a folded postcard. He handed it to Dasie.

Dear Warren,
    I spent the entire day yesterday just stenciling my name on all my possessions believe it or not. Mom's cooking is better except for breakfast, the Navy knows how to put on a good breakfast.
                                                            Sam

P.S. Say Hi to Aunt Betsy & Uncle Frank

"The same, right?" Warren said.

"Exactly. Except for the part about Aunt Betsy and Uncle Frank. Ours said, 'Tell Tattler he's a good dog.'"

Warren laughed.

"What's this?" her father asked.

"Oh, Sam's sending us identical postcards," Dasie explained.

Her dad smiled and leaned the rake against the woodshed. "You know the cure for that, don't you? Start sending him identical letters."

Dasie flushed, suddenly aware she hadn't mailed Sam so much as a postcard herself, even though her mother wrote him almost daily. "The only thing I sent him was those photos. Well, actually Mom mailed those." Her mother had disappeared around the corner in the direction of the vegetable garden. "I guess I don't know what to write. I mean, everything's pretty much the same."

"Nothing wrong with saying so then," her father said. "Sometimes when you're far from home, that's all you really want to hear."

"I just wrote to him last night," Warren said. "I told him about my new job and, uh . . ." He stuck his hands in his pockets and looked suddenly awkward, almost bashful. "And that Mom's letting me have Dad's old motorcycle."

"The hell you say! John's Harley?"

Dasie was at a loss. She'd never heard a word about Uncle John's owning a motorcycle. And she couldn't think when she'd seen her father look more surprised.

"Yeah," Warren said. "Of course there's a couple of strings attached. There usually are with Mom. But she says I can have it."

"I'll be damned," Hank said. "I can't even tell

you when I last laid eyes on that thing. What kind of shape is it in?"

"Well, it needs some work. New tires to start with, then the engine probably needs rebuilding. Oh, and it looks like a family of mice might have made a home out of the seat," he said, smiling. "Except for that, not too much is wrong with it."

"I'll be damned," Dasie's father said again. He took off his cap, scratched his head, and then replaced the cap. "Well, good for you, son. You know, that machine might even be worth some money by now. If you decide you want to sell it, that is."

"Yeah, that's what Mom and Frank said. But right now I just want to get it fixed up, you know?"

"Sure," her father said. Then he shook his head. "I'll tell you what—somewhere I think I have a picture of that bike when it was brand-new. I'll see if I can find it for you."

Late that evening Dasie's father sat down on the dining room sofa with a small carton Dasie recognized as the one she'd seen long ago, containing pictures of Uncle John.

"I still don't understand it," he said. "Years back I tried to talk to Bets about saving that Harley for Warren, but she said no. Insisted she was going to sell it." He opened the top flaps of the carton and pulled out a handful of snapshots. "I thought she *did* sell it, too. You could have knocked me over with a feather when I heard it's been sitting in that garage all these years."

Dasie's mother sat down next to him and watched as he riffled quickly through a pile of photos. Dasie leaned over the sofa arm on the other side.

"It's odd," her mom agreed. "Betsy did nothing but complain about that bike. How many times did she ask John to sell it?"

"About a hundred, I guess," her dad said. He was sifting through photos so fast Dasie could scarcely see them. Some were black-and-white and some color, and she caught mere glimpses of John: posed with a string of fish; with a woman who must have been Betsy, except she was smiling; with a toddler—Warren?—hoisted on his shoulders.

"Well, this may solve a small mystery, though," Dasie's mom said. "A few days back Betsy told me she'd found a way to get Warren to take his G.E.D. exam. Now I'm wondering if she didn't just bribe him with that bike."

Dasie's father harrumphed. "No doubt in my mind. But if Bets thinks this is the first step to prying Warren out of the woods, I'm afraid she's going to be disappointed."

"Yes," her mother said softly, "I expect she will be."

"Ah! Here it is," her dad said. He held up a small snapshot in faded color. Uncle John stood turned slightly away from the shining Harley, washed over in unmistakable joy.

Dasie blinked. At first she thought it was a picture of Warren. The hair was a shade darker and the face somewhat thinner, but in some way—maybe it was the tilt of the head or the shy sideways look at the camera—it was the very image of Warren.

And yet there was something of her father in the photo, too. And of Sam as well. The longer she looked, the harder it was to say exactly who was there.

She held the photo as her father scooped up the other pictures and deposited them back in the carton, quickly closing the flaps.

"He looks so . . . so *young*," Dasie said. "Like he wasn't my uncle at all, but a brother instead."

Her mother slid the picture from her fingers and handed it to her father. He propped it on the shelf against the radio scanner and gazed at it with a look at once distant and filled with longing.

"He was," he said. "He was just young."

When the photo passed to Warren, or whether he saw himself in it as she did, Dasie did not learn. She added this to a growing list of grievances against Mrs. Gower, who was spoiling her days with an ever-growing list of assignments.

By early October homework took up every minute between the end of school and suppertime, and Dasie began to imagine there would be no end to it—that one day she would find she'd finished her homework just in time to return to school the next morning.

The days grew shorter and the nights steadily cooler, but the midday sun remained hot. It was a time of year that Dasie loved, when she could run in the bright heat of an afternoon, yet feel the chill in the air as it brushed past her skin. After school she fought urges to ride out the mill road to Thimbleberry Creek and hunt for bullfrogs, or even just sit under the apple tree in the late afternoons with Warren and her father and listen as they talked about leans and undercuts. The very last place she wanted to be was inside, thinking about grammar.

So when her mother tapped on her door on Saturday morning and said, "How would you like to join me for an outing?" Dasie didn't even ask where to. She was up and dressed in minutes.

They drove east on Old Mill Road, winding past the older houses to the edge of town. In another quarter mile they pulled off to the shoulder. A wrought-iron fence edged the property to their right, and at the center was a broad double gate, chained and padlocked. Just to the side of the double gate was a smaller one, and this stood partly open. Overhead an arch spelled out GRACE FALLS CEMETERY in gold-painted wrought-iron letters, now flecked and peeling with age.

Dasie was spellbound. Countless times she'd come by here on the way in or out of town. But she'd never stopped. Her parents never so much as turned their heads as they drove by, and it had not occurred to Dasie to come on her own, although it would have been mere minutes on her bike.

Her mother opened the trunk of the car and handed Dasie a rake and a spade. Then she hefted a carton with a jumbled assortment of other supplies and led the way through the gate.

They walked up a graveled road, then across an expanse of lawn studded with grave markers. At last they came to an area that was lightly wooded, where grass was a sometime thing. Her mother dropped the carton on the ground at the edge of a ragged border of white-painted river rock. At the far end of the plot a granite marker, ruffled by drying weeds, bore the name clearly—*John Eugene Jenson*. Her uncle John. Dasie stood quietly for a while, letting the sight sink in.

Immediately her mother began shoving the river rocks into an even line. "I've never understood it," she said. "It's like these rocks have a life of their own. They *travel*. Every year I straighten them, and the next year I come back and they've moved. It's the most mysterious thing."

Dasie walked cautiously around her to the next marker. In its polished face was carved *John Henry Jenson*. The date of death was the same year as Dasie's birth. That would have to be her Grandpa Jenson. She hadn't thought of him as having a first name until now. Her grandfather had died when Dasie was six months old. If she tried very hard, would it be possible to remember him? She closed her eyes and reached to the farthest edges of her memory. But nothing came.

"Dasie? It's okay to look around if you want. There's nothing to be afraid of."

"No, I'm not afraid," Dasie said. And she

wasn't. What she was was curious. She walked to the end of the short row of markers, past two more stones bearing the names of Jensons, neither of whom she could place.

Then she set off to cover the length and breadth of the cemetery. She read the name on each marker she passed. Some were names she'd never heard, but others she'd known all her life. There were Lawsons, Blacks, Raineses, Findleys, Williamses, Cabrinis, Ristoes, Wares, and Campbells. Had Monica ever been here? She was a Ristoe.

She reached a back corner of the cemetery, where the grave markers were very old. Most were marble in faint hues of yellow, grey, or pink, and ornate in a way unlike the newer stones. Often there was a verse or message in smaller print below the name. It was almost as though there were fashions in tombstones, she decided, and that this kind had gone out—like mutton sleeves or bustles, or capes for men. It seemed a shame to Dasie. These were somehow soft, inviting to the touch.

On one stone was a dove in flight, and on another hands curved upward in prayer. Dasie lingered for a time over a marker topped by a resting lamb. *Clancey L. Hichet,* it read, *Aged 3 Years, 8 Months, 11 Days.* She ran her fingertips along the lamb's fur, still damp with the last of the morning dew. So many of the tombstones in this part of the cemetery were for children. Dasie walked four rows and circled back, studying dates. In 1887 nine small children had died—three in one family, two in another, and the rest singly. What had happened that year to cause so many deaths?

Farther along were markers for two more Wares and one more Cabrini. Dasie turned and looked around. Why were these family members separate from the others? Then she realized that no marker in this part of the cemetery had a date past 1915. Had this area simply gotten full?

As she crested a small knoll, a singular stone caught her eye. It was taller than most and shaped like the stump of a tree, with a banner wrapped around the top. Across the banner were carved the words *Here Rests a Woodman of the World*. Below, a scroll unfurled. *Eli Eastham, Born Feb. 11, 1863, Died Feb. 17, 1913.*

She made her way back to Uncle John's grave site, where her mother had pulled every weed and was now quickly spading over the surface. She stopped to shake the dirt loose from a clump of volunteer grass. "I want to get this done before someone shows up and sees me digging in the grave-yard," she said, half laughing.

"There's a marker over there, Mom—have you seen it? It's a tree stump."

Her mother smiled. "I've seen it."

"And the other stones?" Dasie said. "I mean, about half the names here I've heard before."

"Mmm. I guess I've seen them all, one time or another." She spaded over the last of the soil, then smoothed it with the back side of the rake. Then she turned the rake around and made neat rows of furrows. Dasie watched her silently, uncertain what the purpose was.

"When I come here, Dasie, I usually stroll around some and pay my respects. Except I think of it more as visiting. Grace Falls has always been a friendly place, and I just kind of think the folks here in the cemetery would appreciate it if someone stopped by once in a while. Spoke a word or two, you know?"

"You stop and *talk*?" Dasie asked, straining at the idea. Her mother was one to take her visiting in small doses. It was hard to picture her as a chatty person. And here of all places! "You talk to everyone? Even the Findleys? I mean, the Findleys are half-crazy! Everybody says so. You never talk to them in town."

"Maybe so," her mother said. She set down the rake and shoved her hair behind her ears. "But I never met the Findleys who are here in the cemetery, so I don't think I should start judging them now. And anyhow, death is a powerful remedy for life."

Dasie's mother pulled a bucket of wildflower seeds from the carton and deliberately sprinkled them across the surface of Uncle John's plot. Then she fell to her knees and began to smooth and pat the earth. Dasie saw the purpose then and joined in, smoothing and patting until the seeds were lightly covered over.

Her mother sat back on her heels and beamed with pleasure. "I wish I'd done this years ago," she said. "I don't know why I didn't think of it.

"I kept trying to decide between roses or bulbs

or just plain grass. Then it hit me. Wildflowers. John loved wildflowers. He'd gather a bunch in the woods on his way home from work and bring them to Betsy in a coffee can full of creek water. The other men ribbed him about it, but it never bothered John."

Dasie could almost see her uncle John as he handed flowers to Aunt Betsy. And she saw Betsy, too, smiling for a wonder.

"What about Aunt Betsy, Mom? Why didn't she plant wildflowers here?"

"Aunt Betsy." Her mother sighed. "Well, if you want the honest truth, I think Betsy's still mad at John for going and getting killed. I'm not sure she ever comes here." She was quiet a minute, then went on. "Anyway, I think this is just easier for me. And I don't mind. It's a labor of love, really."

There was a faint swish of tires as a car passed quickly on the road below. Dasie was reminded again of all the times they'd driven by without stopping. She was suddenly certain that her mother was the only one in their family who came here. It didn't seem right.

"What about Grandma?" she asked. "Didn't she love Uncle John? And Grandpa, too? And why doesn't Dad come here?"

Her mother reached out a hand and stroked her lightly on the cheek. "You need to understand, Dasie, that your grandma's parents are buried here, and a sister and brother, her husband, and a son. It may be just too much grief all in one place."

"Oh," Dasie said. She thought she understood. "Is it the same for Dad, too?"

Her mother hesitated. Then, "No, it's different for your father, Dasie. For your father, his brother exists only in memory. Wherever that memory is, that's where John is. And of course he has hundreds of memories of him—in the house they grew up in, in the woods, in the schools, in the streets of this town. Everywhere. Everywhere except here, that is. He doesn't remember his brother in a cemetery.

"If you ask him, he'll tell you there's no reason to come here, because, for your father, John isn't here."

"But he *is*," Dasie said. Weren't they sitting right beside his grave?

"Not for your father, Dasie. And that's what counts. The thing to understand is that there aren't really any rules about death or about what we believe or what we feel. The only thing that counts is the kindness of understanding."

Dasie folded her arms around her knees and studied the small patch of earth that her mother had just so carefully planted. When the wildflowers came up, nobody in her family would be here to see them except perhaps her mother.

And herself. She made up her mind right then that she'd come back again. For a visit, as her mother would say, though she couldn't quite imagine herself talking to tombstones. But she'd be back.

They sat quietly for a bit longer until her mother said, "Well, I suppose it's time. . . ."

Dasie balanced the rake and spade over one

shoulder and followed her mother down the hill. Twice her mother turned and looked back with a bemused expression. Finally, as they reached the gate, she said, "I'm guessing you didn't see it or you'd have said something."

"See what?" Dasie asked. She turned around. What had she missed?

"Your name," her mother said.

"My . . ."

"I mean, *Dasie Jenson*'s name. That's what I should have said. There was one before you."

"Where?" Dasie asked.

"Up in the old cemetery, just under—"

But Dasie had dropped the rake and spade and was running full tilt up the hill, weaving through grave markers, her feet pounding softly on the grass.

In the old part of the cemetery she skittered from marker to marker, reading quickly. Not there. Not there. Not . . . And then she saw it. A marble tombstone of a buttery white, all but shoved into the foot of a towering cedar. No, it was the other way around. The tree was near to engulfing the stone. A cherub's face, framed by wings, hovered in a cleft at the top.

Dasie B.
Died
May 6, 1879
3 Mo. 17 Ds.
Child of W. E. & A. C. Jenson
Asleep in the Arms of Angels

A baby. A baby named Dasie who'd died more than a hundred years ago. That's why she'd missed it—she'd been looking at ages by then, not names.

For no reason she could have explained, she was suddenly happy. "Hi," she said. "My name is Dasie."

It wasn't a conversation, but it was a start.

EARLY'S SAW SHOP

NICK: *Heard Johnson got thrown out of Skidder's Bar last night.*

DAVE: *Johnson? What'd he do to get throwed out?*

CLAUDE: *Made the mistake of walking in, I expect.*

NICK: *That's about the way they tell it. That kid Lyle was in there, used to work for Johnson. Took a swing at him. Figured he had it coming. Says Johnson cheated him on his scale.*

CLAUDE: *Johnson cheated every cutter ever worked for him.*

DAVE: *Yeah, but you can't prove it. Son of a bitch won't show you his tickets. Says, "You want to see my tickets, you get a court order." Course ain't no logger makes enough money to hire himself a lawyer.*

CLAUDE: *Pat caught him at it once years ago. Ask him. He had a buddy in the log yard, copied the scale off every one of Johnson's tickets for two weeks. Showed it to Pat. Johnson was skimming thirty percent off the top. Put the money in his own pocket.*

DAVE: *That's a dangerous way to live.*

CLAUDE: *Tell me about it.*

NICK: *Well, Skidder told him not to come back.*

Says he's sick of calling the sheriff. Seems like lately every time Johnson walks in the place, he gets drug outside and beat up.

CLAUDE: *The best thing for him.*

seven

"What I wish is that Mrs. Gower would quit giving those pep talks," Dasie said. She and Monica were sprawled on the floor of Monica's bedroom, each with a book in hand.

"I know," Monica said. " 'For high school you'll need to know this. For college you'll need to know that.' Like it's all going to happen tomorrow, and if we don't learn this stuff right away, we'll be dog food. I hate it."

"Today when she said, 'As adults you will find that bad grammar makes a bad impression,' " Dasie said, in what she thought was a pretty good imitation of Mrs. Gower's gravelly voice, "I just thought to myself, Then I'm in no particular hurry to be one."

Monica laughed. "Yeah, like what's the rush, right?" Then she added more soberly, "At the beginning of the year you know she actually scared me? I'm getting more used to her, though."

"Me, too," Dasie admitted. She still didn't like all the homework. But now that the days were shorter, it didn't seem so unnatural to be inside. It was the end of the first week in November, and already there'd been one good rain. Every morning and most evenings her parents built a small fire in the woodstove to take off the chill.

It had been Monica's suggestion that they start doing their homework together, and Dasie was grateful. She needed help with decimals anyhow, and Monica was an ace at math. And they both needed encouragement for the report on "Our State's Historical Figures."

They read quietly for several more minutes, then Monica said, "This is such a yawner!" and slammed her book shut.

"Come on," Dasie said. "We have to do this. We said we'd read for an hour, and it's been what, twenty minutes?"

"I can't read this," Monica said. "Why did I ever choose Mark Hopkins for my report, of all people? He's so boring. It's just railroads and money, money and railroads. I hate it."

Dasie sighed. "Fremont's no better," she said. "He supposedly discovered a lot of places, but so far all he does is march around with this army, dragging a howitzer everywhere."

"What's a howitzer?"

"A cannon. Imagine that, walking around on a perfectly nice day, dragging a cannon!" She slammed her book shut too, and giggled.

"I thought of asking Mrs. Gower if I could choose someone else," Monica said.

"It's too late," Dasie said. "I already tried. I told her I'd rather do a report on someone I could understand. You know, an ordinary person with an ordinary life, like you or me, but they just happened to live a long time ago?"

"So what did she say?"

"She said that wasn't the point." Dasie sighed. "You know where I'd like to be? Down on Thimbleberry Creek by the beaver pond. I bet the swans are there right now."

"Oh! Did you hear them circling over town last night? They were calling and calling."

"I know," Dasie said. "I could hardly sleep. Sam told me the reason they do that on a cloudy night is they can't see to land. They know there's water down here somewhere, but they just can't find it."

"Mmm," Monica said. And then, while Dasie was still thinking of swans, she said, "How's Sam doing anyhow?"

"Okay, I guess. He keeps sending postcards. Now he's saying he's going to study electronics. Aviation electronics. Something like that."

Monica hiked herself up and leaned her back against the bed frame. She fidgeted with a shoelace and said, "I guess Warren misses him, huh?"

There was something about her voice that raised little prickles on the back of Dasie's neck. She hadn't seen a whole lot of Warren lately. True, he did come by for an hour or so every few days to see her father.

But they mostly sat on the back porch and talked about logging or the fire department. Dasie usually just said hello and passed them by. Then Warren went home. She knew he worked some every night on the Harley.

"Of course Warren misses him," she said. "We all do. Mom more than any of us maybe, but after that probably Warren misses him most."

"Okay," Monica said. "Just wondering."

Wondering. "Monica! How can you wonder? You know they were always together."

"I know. But I just thought now that Warren and Amy have this *thing*, maybe Warren isn't so sorry Sam is gone."

"Amy? Amy Ware?" Dasie's mind raced. Warren and Amy? That wasn't possible. Warren wouldn't be going out with Amy. No way. "It isn't true. Whatever you heard, it's wrong," she said.

Monica remained resolutely fixed on her shoelaces. She neither spoke nor looked at Dasie.

"Monica?"

Monica shrugged.

Dasie gathered up her books and walked out the door.

By the time she reached the back gate at home, she felt foolish. And a little sheepish. It wasn't fair to get mad at Monica just because someone had told her something and she'd repeated it.

Dasie's mother was just headed toward the back door with an armload of wood when Dasie walked through the gate. She raced for the door and held it for her mother. "Where's Dad?" Dasie asked. Her father usually kept the wood box full.

"He and Warren left a couple of hours ago to go out to a job site. I guess Warren walked off the job early today after some beef with Johnson about a tree. I didn't catch all of it, but whatever it is, your father wanted to see for himself." She dropped the wood in the box with a clatter. "It'll probably be good and dark before they get back. It's way out by Panther Gulch somewhere."

Dasie left her books on the kitchen table and went to the phone in the dining room. She dialed Monica's number.

"Sorry about that," she said.

"No problem," Monica said.

"Well, I shouldn't have gotten mad at you, that's all."

"That's okay, I understand," she said.

"Well. I'd come back over, but Mom's here alone. Dad and Warren are off somewhere looking at trees."

"Mmm."

"So I'll see you in school tomorrow?" Dasie said.

"Sure," Monica said, "same as always."

Dasie was sorry she'd thrown in that bit about where Warren was. She'd only done it to prove he wasn't out with Amy. And that was silly. She didn't have to prove anything about some story someone was telling.

She picked up her books and went to her room. Her mother gave her a questioning look as she passed through the kitchen, but Dasie pretended not to notice. Some stories weren't worth repeating.

She kicked her shoes off, climbed on her bed, and leaned against the headboard. She knew she should really read more about Fremont, but it was the last thing she wanted to do.

Now, a history of the first Dasie B. Jenson, that would be interesting. How did she happen to get born and die in Grace Falls anyhow? The immigrant trail to Oregon passed over the mountains just forty miles from Grace Falls. Had baby Dasie's parents been on the way to Oregon and maybe just got sick of walking about the time they got near here? Or did they stop because a baby was on the way?

Dasie had returned once to the cemetery, and she'd figured out that baby Dasie was the first Jenson buried in Grace Falls. Or the first with a marker anyhow. And she hadn't yet found markers for W. E. and A. C. Jenson.

She'd taken with her a large sheet of butcher paper that she'd gotten from Bill Reed down at Gifford's Market, a black oil chalk from the art shelf in the school library, and some masking tape. She'd taped the paper over the tombstone and made a rubbing. The cherub had not turned out well, but the words were clear. The rubbing was now tacked to the wall across from Dasie's bed.

She picked up a notebook and pen and began a letter to Sam. She told him all about the marker for baby Dasie and everything she knew about her, which so far wasn't much. Then she told him about the swans. Then she signed her name. She looked at the page, which was nearly full of script, the most she'd written to Sam since he left. Then she added a P.S.: *Do you ever hear from Amy?*

It was well after dark when her father got home. By then Dasie had helped her mother with the evening's fire. She twisted a paper grocery sack, wrapped it in a cardboard egg carton, and set it in the bottom of the stove. Over this they stacked as many pieces of lodgepole pine as would fit. Her mother opened the flues, struck a match, and closed the stove door. Then she and Dasie stood with their backs to the growing fire and watched the clock. A large beef-and-vegetable lasagna was warming in the oven.

Finally Tattler set up a barking, and they heard the engine of her father's pickup truck. A minute later his feet clomped on the back porch, and then he was in the kitchen, swearing.

"That damned Johnson! That old son of a bitch! If ever a man shouldn't be let to die in his sleep, it's him." He yanked open the refrigerator door and pulled out two bottles of beer, then sat in his chair at the table and glowered. He made no move to open the beer.

"What happened?" "Is Warren okay?" Both Dasie and her mother spoke at once.

Hank pulled a hand over his face. "The only one that showed good sense was Warren," he said. He shook his head in disbelief. "He had a big ol' Doug fir with a cat face in the stump. Course Warren didn't know it would fall any different from any other tree. It's a common enough mistake for a youngster, but in Johnson's outfit nobody teaches you anything. Nobody knows enough *to* teach.

"So Warren just went ahead as usual. He put in his Humboldt undercut, but what he didn't know was that he'd need to put in a standard undercut, too. So when he puts in his back cut, the edge of that cat face hits first, and the Doug fir takes a spin and ends hung up, dead center, right in the middle of a ponderosa pine.

"Johnson comes along, sees this, and throws a fit. Tells Warren to get that tree on the ground or he'll never work for another logging outfit. Well, Warren's already looked it over and talked to a couple of the other guys, but not one of them is anything but *guessing* how to get both those trees down without getting killed. The top of that pine is bent right over with the weight of that Doug fir. Johnson's hollering at him, and Warren calculates the kind of pressure must be in that stump, and he gets the shakes. And I mean gets 'em bad. Picks up his saw and leaves. Which I told him is the first sign of good sense.

"Last words Warren hears as he walks down the hill is, 'You're fired, Jenson!' He drove straight here. Says to me that even though he's fired, he's the one that hung up that tree, and it'll be his fault if someone gets hurt trying to get it down. So he wants me to tell him how. I believe he meant to drive back out there and do it himself. But I told him a hung tree is *always* a two-person job. One of you has to be watching the tops the whole time.

"Well, we go out there together, maybe only forty minutes of daylight left, and it's still sitting there. But worse than I imagined. First thing we did was clear brush about a hundred feet in both directions, so we'd have plenty of room to run. Then I had Warren put his undercut in the ponderosa pine. Easy like. Real easy. And I'm watching the top of that Doug fir in case it shifts. When the undercut's in, I go around and bore into the back side. You don't want to make a back cut, 'cause a point will come where that pine's gonna barber chair on you, and if it doesn't catch you snapping back, the Doug fir'll crush you. Either way, there's no walking away alive. So what I showed Warren was how to bore out the guts and just leave a lip.

"But I'll tell you, I got the cold sweats. It's been a long time since I've sweated like that. All that weight hanging by just a thin rim of wood. Man!

"I let Warren do the last part. He was standing on one side, I was on the other, and when he was ready, he fired up his saw. He touched that lip and *bam!* Just like a gunshot. He threw his saw and ran one way, and I ran the other. We neither of us looked back. And the noise! It was just one continuous roar until they hit the ground, those trees taking out everything in their path. I never stopped running until the noise stopped.

"When we went back to look, you coulda landed a seven-forty-seven in the path that was cleared. I expect it's gonna take the best part of the day tomorrow just to clean up the cripples."

Dasie listened to all of this as though time had stopped. If she'd breathed, she didn't know it. She looked at her mother, who sat with her hands pressed tight over her mouth.

Her father's knuckles were white around one of the unopened bottles of beer. He twisted the top off and took a long swig. Then he just shook his head.

Her mother slumped back in her chair. "It scares the life out of me for Warren to be falling," she said. "I don't often side with Betsy, but to tell the truth, I can't say I'm sorry he's fired."

Dasie's father harrumphed. "He's not fired. Johnson gets out there tomorrow and sees those trees on the ground and nobody dead, he'll be begging to have Warren back. I told him just to pack his lunch and show up same as usual."

"Oh, no!" her mother said. "Oh, Hank, for just a minute there I thought, Warren's safe—he's out of it. How could you send him back after today?"

Dasie's father took a while answering. He pulled again at his beer and then set it down and turned it slowly by the neck, studying the label. Then he pushed it aside and bent forward, unlacing his boots. When he sat upright, he said, "I'll tell you, Anne, until today I'd have agreed with you. I *did* agree with you. But today I realized Warren's going to make a timber faller.

"No thanks to Johnson, you understand. Next time I see Johnson I'll be resisting a powerful urge to alter the placement of his nose. But Warren's got a feel for timber falling. He's got the instincts. And he has the respect. From now on I'll worry less about Warren than I did before."

Dasie took a deep breath and let it out. Her father had his steely side, but it was a thoughtful kind of steel. If he said Warren could do this job, then he could do it. Plain as plain.

But her mother wasn't convinced. Her brow furrowed in concentration. "Couldn't you get him a job at the mill, Hank? At least there he'd get proper training."

Dasie's father raised his eyebrows. "At the mill? No, I could not. In the first place they're not hiring. In fact, there's rumors of layoffs every day. And in the second place the mill's no guarantee against injury. How many people do you know in this town missing fingers or had a hand cut off and sewed back on? And last year Joey Dirico got his leg crushed and near ripped off, remember."

Dasie's mother covered her face with her hands. "Stop," she whispered. "Please stop."

Her father sighed. "I'm sorry," he said. "I know you don't like to hear about this stuff. And you're right, it's a lot more dangerous to work in the woods than it is in the mill. But I guess what I'm trying to say is you've got to be careful either way. And a little bit lucky, too."

"Okay," Dasie's mom said, "I understand that. But I guess I'd worry less if Warren was in the mill, that's all."

"Except for thing number three," her dad said, "which is that Warren would never go. I think we need to just accept that his mind is made up." He picked up his boots, carried them to the dining room, and set them by the stove. Dasie's mother stood and pulled the lasagna dish from the oven.

When Dasie's dad returned, he said, "And I might as well admit that when I was out there today, I got to thinking I wouldn't halfway mind going back to timber falling myself."

"You wouldn't!" said her mother.

"No." He laughed. "No, I would not. For the simple reason I don't run as fast as I used to."

Over the next ten days, Grace Falls took a steep slide toward real winter. Dasie needed her jacket on the way to school each day, and there was no longer a night without a fire in the stove. One day she woke up, and there was hardly a leaf left on the apple tree. Her father got out his Hubbard's shoe grease and coated both pairs of his work boots against the winter wet, then set them by the stove to dry.

The fire department was having its busy season. Dinner was interrupted on three separate nights by flue fires in different parts of town. Each time her father came back annoyed at how some folks had to wait for a fire to decide to have their chimney pipes cleaned.

On the fourteenth of November, Dasie stayed up late to finish her report on Fremont, then read it in class the next day. When Mrs. Gower told her she'd done a good job, she felt guilty for not having tried harder.

Snow began to fall at noon in small dry flakes, swirling past the school windows on a cold wind. There was more than an inch on the ground by the end of school.

Dasie went straight home, feeling cold and tired. In the yard Tattler tore up and down. He always ran like mad in the snow, as though chasing something, or as though something was chasing him. She watched him for a minute, then went in, grateful for the bank of warm air she met inside the back door.

When her mother asked her to go to the post office for the mail, Dasie very nearly refused. But it was only a five-minute round trip. She exchanged her light jacket for her heavy down one, took the postbox key from inside the utility closet door, and headed off for Main Street.

The post office lobby was empty and strangely hot. Dasie pulled the mail from their box—two bills, two catalogs, one circular, and a postcard from Sam, addressed to her. She stuffed the postcard in her side pocket to save for later and pushed out the door.

A dark green pickup truck pulled in front of the post office just as Dasie got outside. For a second it looked only vaguely familiar. Then the horn honked, and she realized it was Warren. She smiled and raised her hand. That's when she saw Amy, sitting not by the passenger door but smack up next to Warren on the middle of the bench seat. Dasie's hand fell, and she turned toward home, feeling flushed, queasy, and light-headed.

So it was true after all. Warren had actually stolen her brother's girl. She walked home in an enveloping heat that seemed to start at her feet and rise to her head. Her heart, she knew, was pounding. She could feel it twisting into a hard, mean knot against Warren, and Dasie just let it. Sam had always been more than a cousin to Warren. He was his most loyal supporter, his truest friend. Sam loved Warren. And he trusted him.

Inside the house Dasie had only time enough to get her coat off and make it to the bathroom before she threw up.

eight

By noon the following day there was no trace of the snow. It had been only a warning. Dasie remained in bed all that day and the two that followed, racked with fever and chills. The flu, her mother said—it was going around town. She lined Dasie's bedside table with a tempting parade of liquids, but nothing stayed down for long, and Dasie slept fitfully between bouts of nausea.

When she woke on the fourth day, her fever was gone, though she felt limp, wrung out. She moved on wobbly legs to the dining room sofa so her mother could change her bed and air the room. She spent the morning there, reading, spooning in Jell-O, and nibbling cautiously on saltine crackers as a fire whispered softly in the woodstove. Then she drifted off to sleep just past noon.

This sleep was deep and peaceful, and it was nearing dark when she woke. The stove was making small popping sounds, the way it did when the fire got low. Dasie knew immediately she was alone in the house. She wrapped herself in the afghan and went in search of her mother.

She found her sitting on the top step of the back porch, bundled in a heavy sweater, her hands tucked under her arms. Wisps of hair had worked loose from her ponytail and blew slantwise in the wind.

"Mom?"

Her mother rose quickly. "Oh, Dasie, you shouldn't be out here. It's cold."

"I was just wondering where you were," Dasie said. "I feel better, but I'm all sticky. Do you think it's okay to take a bath?"

Her mother laid a hand against her forehead, testing, then pulled the afghan higher around her neck. "Sure, a bath is fine. But don't get chilled, okay? I left a clean nightie on your bed."

Dasie looked around. She still didn't understand. "Why are you sitting out here?" she asked.

"Oh, Dasie, it's . . . I saw Lorraine Cabrini at the market, and she told me. . . . I don't know if it's true. But there was going to be a big meeting at the mill at the end of the shift today."

"If what's true?" Dasie asked. It was long past the time for the mill whistle. Her mother was making no sense. And she hadn't looked so distracted since . . . well, since the log-yard fire. "Is Dad okay?"

"I don't know," her mother said. "I hope so." Then she turned toward Dasie and saw her widening eyes. "Oh, no, I mean he's okay, Dasie. I just don't know whether . . ." At that moment they both heard the engine of her father's truck.

"Scoot," her mother said. "Go get your bath." And then she bolted down the steps and across the lawn.

Dasie retreated a couple of steps toward the door but did not go in. She watched as her mother fumbled with the gate latch and reached her father's truck just as his door opened. Something was very wrong. For two or three minutes they spoke while her father sat behind the wheel. Then he climbed down and pulled a folded paper from his back pocket. His head hung and his shoulders sagged as Dasie's mother scanned the page. Finally they put their arms around each other, and although she'd never seen her father cry, Dasie knew unmistakably that he was crying now. She turned and slipped into the house.

She stayed a long time in the tub, watching curls of steam rise in the air. If she stayed there long enough, she hoped, whatever was wrong would be over and done with when she got out.

But it wasn't. She found her parents seated silently at the kitchen table, a rumpled pink paper spread between them.

Her mother caught her eye. "You may as well read it," she said. "It concerns us all."

Dasie read quickly, skipping. *All Hourly and Salaried Employees . . . cease operations effective January 3rd . . . unavailability of resources . . .*

*declining revenues . . . no longer feasible . . . sever-
ance pay . . .* She looked up. "The mill's closing?
For good?"

Her mother nodded. Dasie's head suddenly
flooded with questions. Who decided? Would they
change their minds? What about all those logs
stacked in the yard? And what would her father do
in the morning instead of walking out the door with
his lunch pail in hand? He had never missed a day
of work in all of Dasie's remembered life.

She couldn't muster the strength to ask a single
one of her questions. Instead she found herself wish-
ing she hadn't long ago outgrown sitting on laps.
She walked over to her father, leaned into his shoulder, and put an arm around his neck.

A silence settled over Grace Falls. It was unlike
anything Dasie had ever known. For days it was as
though the entire town had lost the power of speech.
At the post office people passed in and out with
their heads down. At Gifford's Market neighbors
avoided one another's eyes. The friendly waves from
passing cars vanished.

But a new kind of communication sprang up to
take the place of spoken words. Dasie saw grown-
ups reach out in passing to squeeze a hand, then
move on. More than once she felt the gentle pressure
of an adult hand on her shoulder, only to turn and
see the retreating back of a familiar figure.

In school she could look around the classroom
and count seven kids whose parents worked at the

mill. And she saw some of those kids doing the same thing—looking around. Looking at her. Without explaining, she stopped going to Monica's after school to do homework. Monica didn't ask why. She knew. Her father ran the forklift at the mill.

Dasie's parents didn't talk about the mill closing, at least not around her. But neither did they talk much about anything else. They walked through the house as though a sick person were sleeping in the next room, avoiding any noise that might make a disturbance. But after she'd gone to bed at night, Dasie heard mumblings of quiet conversation that lasted until she drifted off to sleep.

The spell of silence broke on Friday afternoon. When Dasie came in the back door, her mother was chopping celery, and a big kettle of stew simmered on the stove. The table was covered with tidy stacks of papers—bills and bank statements, canceled checks, and cash register receipts. Usually Dasie saw these things only a few at a time, when her mother sat down on payday to pay the bills. A large ledger lay open in front of her mother's chair with column after column of figures in her small, neat hand.

"What are you working on?" Dasie asked.

Her mom smiled. "Once upon a time I used to keep good records of everything we spent. Every penny, Dasie. It's time I started doing it again. We're going to need to figure out a way to live on less money."

Dasie hung her sweatshirt on a hook by the door, put her books on a chair, and sat in her mother's seat. She scanned quickly down the page in front of her. Everything was there, from laundry soap to postage stamps to Tattler's rabies tag. "This all looks like necessary stuff," she said.

Her mother scraped the celery from the cutting board into the stew pot. "Well, it's not every bit as necessary as it looks," she said. "There are things we could do without. Like cable TV, for instance."

"Cable! Mom, without cable we get exactly one channel!"

Her mother cocked her head at her and raised an eyebrow. "Don't you think I know that? Now, Dasie, I'm not saying we'll definitely get rid of cable, but we may have to if we want to stay here."

Dasie sucked in her breath. "Stay? You mean stay in this house?"

"In this house and in Grace Falls," her mother said. She stirred the stew gently with a wooden spoon. "Your father and I have been talking, and that's what we want to do if we can manage. We don't want to leave your Grandma Jenson alone, for one thing, and we really can't uproot her. All of her friends, her whole life is here."

Dasie slumped against the back of the chair. Leave Grace Falls? She'd tried to guess what kind of work her father would do when the mill closed and had got no further than thinking maybe there'd be a job at the gas station. But leaving had never crossed her mind. "All my friends are here, too," she said. It came out as a whisper.

"I know that," her mother said. "And my friends

are here, and your father's friends. But we're young enough. If we have to make new friends someplace else, we can do it."

Dasie was quiet for several minutes while her mother stirred and sampled the stew. "I guess I just don't want to leave," she said at last. "I like it here. I'm used to it, you know?"

"I know," her mother said. She laid the spoon on the stove. "We like it, too. That's why we want to stay. But it may not be possible. And even if we do stay, it won't be the same, Dasie. Grace Falls won't be the same. The mill *is* this town, and without it the town will change."

This seemed wrong to Dasie. The town was more than the mill. It was the houses and the streets and the post office and Gifford's Market, and the fire department, and Early's, and all their friends and neighbors. The mill was a big part, but it was only one part. Staying was what mattered. "I guess we don't really have to have cable TV," she said. "I mean, big deal, lots of times we don't even have time to watch it."

Her mother smiled warmly. "That's my girl," she said.

Dasie walked down First Street the next morning under a threatening sky. The wind blew from the southeast, sending dry leaves racing past her feet. In one hand, clutched in a pocket, she held a round wooden token, two inches in diameter, worn to an oily smoothness with age.

One of her earliest memories was of walking down First Street, holding onto her mother with one hand and a token just like this with the other. Carrying it had made her feel important, trusted. When they arrived at the market, Dasie had solemnly handed the token to Bill, the butcher, who, in turn, handed her mother a turkey not much smaller than Dasie herself.

As she grew bigger and the turkeys smaller, Dasie was allowed to go alone to get the turkey, and long after the novelty wore off, it still felt like an honor. This year was different, though. Her father had flipped the token once in the air before handing it to Dasie, saying, "I guess this is the last time we'll see one of these."

In line at the butcher counter Dasie pulled the token from her pocket and turned it in her hand. Burned into one side was the number fourteen, on the other the letters *GFLC*. It was a tradition dating back to the earliest days of the Grace Falls Lumber Company, to the time when Mother Grace provided every family in town with a Thanksgiving turkey. Even when Consolidated Timber took over, the tokens had remained for mill workers. One year the company substituted small certificates with the Consolidated Timber logo on the top, but the old-timers raised a fuss, and the next year the tokens were back.

When her turn came, Dasie handed the token to Bill. "Mom likes the hens best," she said.

"Largest hen I've got left is fourteen pounds, two ounces, Dasie. Will that do you?"

Dasie nodded. With Sam away, it would just be the three of them this year, plus Grandma Jenson. Betsy, Frank, and Warren would be driving to Portland to spend the holiday with Betsy's sister, and Dasie's San Francisco grandparents only made the trip every third year at most.

Bill wrapped the turkey in white butcher paper, scrawled *CT* in black crayon across the breast, and handed it to Dasie. Then he held out the token. "I got the number off this. Company says you can keep it if you want."

Dasie hesitated.

"Kind of like a remembrance," he urged.

She took the token and stuffed it back in her pocket.

Monica was at the end of the line as Dasie passed. "Wait for me?" she asked.

Dasie stood outside the sliding glass doors, the turkey cradled in her arms, until Monica arrived; then they cut across to First Street and turned north. The wind had lessened, but a light rain splattered the pavement.

"We're leaving," Monica said.

"Oh, Monica, no! You mean moving?"

"Uh-huh."

"Oh, you *can't*," Dasie said. "You just can't. It's not fair."

"That's what *I* said, but Dad says we don't have

any choice. His cousin Clay found him work driving a forklift in Stockton, and he says if he doesn't take it, he may not find another job."

Dasie stopped in her tracks. Words her father had spoken the previous night came rushing back—how he wasn't qualified for any job that wasn't either in a sawmill or the woods, and how the mills that were still open didn't need any saw filers. He said there wasn't much sense in leaving when there was no work for him someplace else. Maybe Monica was lucky her dad drove a forklift.

"Stockton's so far, though," she said.

"I know," Monica said. "And the schools are huge, and I may have to ride a bus, and there might be gangs . . . and I won't know *anybody*." She was suddenly sobbing.

Dasie set the turkey right down in the road where she stood and put her arms around her friend. "The bus won't be too bad," she said. It sounded weak, but it was all she could think of to say.

Monica shook her head. "The worst thing is we have to leave before Christmas. Mom and Dad are home right now, cleaning things out so we can pack."

"Before Christmas? Oh, Monica!" Dasie was afraid she might cry, too, and then what would they do?

Two cars came by, making wide arcs to avoid them, but Monica didn't seem to notice and Dasie never moved. Finally Dasie said, "I'll come visit you." She had no idea how she would accomplish this. She only knew that someday she would.

Before Thanksgiving a FOR SALE sign was posted in front of the Ristoe house. And another stood in front of the Cabrini house on First Street. Danny had gotten a job pulling green chain at a mill in Placerville. It was the bottom of the heap as mill-work went—backbreaking labor pulling wet and heavy boards off the conveyor—but he figured he was young enough to work his way back up. Dasie's father only shook his head and said, "The fire department will miss him."

Horace Perkins had decided simply to retire from his post as night watchman. He said he'd worn out all his joints on his way to the watchman's job, and he was too old to learn anything new.

On Thanksgiving morning Dasie held tight to the turkey hen while her mother stuffed the cavities. The stuffing had celery and frozen corn but no oysters. Oysters were on the list of things not really necessary.

In the living room her father watched a pregame football show. Dasie decided if you didn't look too closely, it would have seemed like any other Thanks-giving, with Tattler hovering in the kitchen and the TV chattering in the background. But her father's left knee bounced up and down, and her mother kept losing her place in the order of cooking.

Grandma Jenson's arrival settled them all down

a bit. She brought a pie and sweet potatoes and a bottle of sherry, which only she drank. But still Dasie wished that this year had not been one of their smaller Thanksgivings. A commotion might have hidden the worry.

The brightest moment came when Sam telephoned. As Dasie listened to her father talk, she realized that until then Sam had not been told of the mill closing.

Her dad was making the best of things: "No, no, son, we're going to be fine. We haven't quite worked out all the ifs, ands, and buts yet. But we will. And you know your old man—hard work never scared me."

Grandma Jenson took the phone and asked Sam all manner of questions. Had he learned how to march? Had he made friends? Where were they from? Was he warm enough at night? When she started asking the same questions a second time, Dasie understood it was the sound of his voice she wanted, not his answers.

Then even Tattler had his turn. Dasie's mom held the receiver toward him as Sam whistled and shouted until finally Tattler's tail waved in circles and he barked *Arf!* over and over.

At last it was Dasie's turn. "I wish you were here," she said.

"Me, too," Sam said. "I stood in line for an hour at one phone, and then I walked almost half a mile to get to this one. There was nobody here, and now—do you believe it, Dasie?—there are four guys waiting!"

"You won't hang up!" she said.

"No, not right away. But, Dasie, is everyone really okay?"

Dasie looked around at the smiling, expectant faces of her family. "Kinda," she said. "Sorta." She paused a moment, then said, "Did Mom tell you she's looking for a job in Morgantown?"

"Yeah . . . ," he said. "How's she doing, really? The truth, Dasie—is she coming unglued?"

"No," Dasie said. Then, lowering her voice, she said, "That's what's weird, Sam. She's fine. It's Dad who's not himself. Half the time it's like part of him isn't here."

There was a silence in which Dasie could hear a muffled roar in the background punctuated by the honking of car horns. "Well," Sam said, "I guess that's understandable. He's lived for that mill for years."

"Yeah, I guess so," Dasie said.

"How 'bout you?" Sam asked. "Are you okay?"

"I don't know," Dasie admitted. "I just wish I knew what to expect. Some people are moving away. Monica's leaving." She took a deep breath.

"I'm sorry," Sam said. Then, "Look, I know this must be rough, but you can handle it, Dasie. Remember, you're strong."

"I'm not so sure anymore."

"Well, *I'm* sure. It'll all work out, Dasie, promise." He sounded so far away. For a moment there was nothing on the line but a faint din of voices and traffic. Then he said, "So what do you want for Christmas?"

"Nothing," Dasie answered. "Just come home. That's all."

nine

Dasie's mother had the *Morgantown Weekly* spread open on the dining room sofa while Dasie sat cross-legged on the floor, doodling in the margins of her notebook. The doodles were of holly leaves and berries, a border of them stretching around three sides of the page, the way Christmas lights would border a porch.

Except that her family had not strung Christmas lights across the front porch this year. Nor had almost anyone else in town. When Dasie asked about it, her mother said, "Somehow it just doesn't seem right to make a big fuss over Christmas with so many people about to lose their jobs. You know?"

Dasie knew. All anyone could talk about anymore was what would happen when the mill closed, what had begun to happen already. It was hard to keep your mind on anything else, even Christmas.

And especially homework. Dasie's math book lay open on the floor in front of her, ignored. The whole reason for homework was to help you get good grades so you could get into college and someday get a job outside of Grace Falls. But that was the one thing everyone was most upset about—having to leave Grace Falls. So what was the point?

In class that morning Mrs. Gower had asked how many knew for certain their families would be moving. Four hands went up. She made a sucking noise through her teeth, wrote quickly on a piece of paper, then said, "I think it's best that we all expect some changes. If enrollment falls too far, the county board will have to close this school and bus our students to Morgantown."

There were gasps and groans all around the room, and for once Mrs. Gower made no objection. She sank into her chair, spread her fingers on the desk, and stroked the shiny wooden surface while Dasie's classmates talked among themselves.

Nobody wanted to go to school in Morgantown. It wasn't just that they wouldn't be able to walk home for lunch or play sports after school, or that classes would be bigger. The trouble was the Morgantown kids and the way they looked down their noses at you if you were from Grace Falls, like there was something wrong if your parents got dirty when they went to work. Who would want to go to school with people who looked down their noses?

On the sofa Dasie's mother snipped at the paper with her scissors. "If you give up reading the want ads and start looking at the business advertisements, there are lots of people who might need help. Like here's the dry cleaner's. I could work there. How hard could that be?

"Oh, and here's Tucker Painting. Housepainting. Your father could do that. He's painted this whole house twice. As long as he was *moving,* he'd be okay."

"Mmm," Dasie said. Already she'd learned not to get too involved in her mother's musings. Her mom had a new idea about jobs almost daily but so far had gotten only one interview—along with a dozen other people—for a job as a clerk in a fabric store.

Dasie was working on a second row of holly leaves, now aiming for a continuous border that would end at the center of the page, when her father came in from fire drill. He didn't greet anyone, but hung his turnouts in the utility closet, then stood for a long time in front of the stove, warming his hands. Finally he said, "Polly turned in her resignation tonight."

"No!" "Oh, no." Dasie and her mother both spoke at once.

"She's taking a job as sheriff's dispatcher in Faro, starting the end of January."

Dasie's mother folded the paper and put it aside. "Well, that's actually the perfect job for Polly," she said. "But still, I can't believe it. Polly Ware has been here forever. She's not really going to sell her house and move, is she?"

"No," he said. "Harry and Marsha left her that house outright. She'll never sell. But she is going to close it up for the winter. Polly doesn't want to try to travel over those roads once the snow comes, and she doesn't really like Amy driving back and forth either. They'll get a little apartment in Faro. Or a trailer. Something."

Dasie wondered what Warren would think of this. She'd never said a word to her parents about Warren and Amy, and she didn't know whether they even knew, though Warren and Amy were at no great pains to keep their romance secret. Just this afternoon she'd seen them drive out of town together in the direction of the falls.

As if he'd heard her thoughts, her father said, "And Warren missed drill tonight. Did he call here?"

"No," Dasie said.

"No," her mother echoed. "Although I did have a call from Betsy this morning. She invited us up there for an early supper Saturday."

"Huh," her father said, in a voice Dasie took to mean "that's strange." He stood rubbing his hands for a minute, then said it again. "Huh."

It *was* strange when Dasie considered how little time they spent with Aunt Betsy and Uncle Frank. In the last year or so it had been mostly holidays— Easter and Christmas. And Christmas was only three weeks away.

Saturday morning Dasie and her father picked up their Forest Service permits—one for them and one for Grandma Jenson—and drove out in search of Christmas trees. This was usually a happy occasion, but today the drive was almost somber. Her father was all business, thinking out loud about where the nearest spot would be to get a good enough tree and get back.

All at once Dasie missed Sam more than ever. It was Sam who made the most of the hunt, leading them farther and farther into the woods in search of just the right tree and laughing off complaints about how far they'd have to drag it back to the truck. She thought about how they all talked about what Sam was doing in Chicago, the classes he was taking, the colds he caught one after another, but how nobody actually asked him if he minded being away from Grace Falls. She was suddenly sure he did.

They picked a small tree for Grandma Jenson and a larger one for themselves—though not as large as some they'd had—and left each standing in a bucket of water in the side yard while they cleaned up for supper and drove the three blocks to Betsy and Frank's house.

The house, a pale yellow with white trim, stood in the middle of the last block of Spruce Street. Warren came down the short drive to meet them, then led them back to the garage, eager to show off his work on the Harley. It was still partly in pieces, the rear tire off and no seat in sight, but every bit of the metalwork gleamed. Betsy and Frank came out while Dasie's father asked questions about the engine and said, "Good enough!" or "Good for you!" to every answer.

Inside they all milled about the kitchen for a while until dinner was served. With some surprise Dasie became aware that something had changed. Aunt Betsy was unsmiling as ever, but there was a softness to her, as though she'd lost her quills. She asked Dasie about school and accepted her mother's help with the gravy for the roast. Uncle Frank made a remark about the 49ers, and soon he and her father were standing off to the side, drinking beer and making football predictions.

Warren seemed . . . just Warren. He made a teasing remark about how Dasie's hair was growing out, but she hung back. There was still that knot in her chest.

Aunt Betsy had outdone herself. The dining table was set with her best dishes on a pale yellow linen cloth. There were even candles in silver candlesticks, though Dasie noticed they were never lit.

Dinner was served, the food consumed, and chairs pushed back from the table when Frank cleared his throat. "Bets and me, we need to tell you . . . well, her brother-in-law offered me a job in Portland. Driving a gravel truck. His company's doing real well, and it'd be good steady work. I— Bets and me, that is—we've been talking it over, and I think I'd better take it. Being as how things are."

Dasie glanced around. Warren was studying his

lap, and her parents showed no surprise. When it came down to it, Dasie wasn't surprised either, though she couldn't say why. Maybe she was losing the gift for surprise—so much was changing so fast.

Right away her mom murmured, "Oh, Bets, we'll miss you," and her dad said, "They'll be getting a good man, Frank. Course we'll be losing one, but I'm sure this is the right decision."

"Yes, but it's Warren we worry about," Betsy said.

"*I'm* not worried, it's them," Warren said. He was scowling.

"Warren has decided not to come with us," Frank explained. "Not yet anyhow. He has his job here, at least until we get some snow and the woods close. And then he's promised to study for his G.E.D. exam in the spring. Course I told him with the mill closing Johnson Logging's like to go under, but Warren thinks they'll last. Leastaways he wants to hang on till spring."

"If things don't work out by then, he'll come up to Portland and maybe go to a junior college," Betsy said. There was a catch in her voice, and Dasie saw she was close to tears.

Dasie's father cleared his throat and said, "Well, I'd be inclined to agree with Frank, Warren. I don't think Johnson can last without Consolidated Timber."

"Maybe not," Warren said, "but maybe come spring I can get on with a bigger outfit."

Dasie's father shook his head, but before he

could speak again Frank said, "Point is, we've talked this all over, and Warren's set on staying. So what we're wondering is, could he stay with you folks? His mother . . . *we'd* feel better knowing he was looked after."

Dasie's parents didn't so much as miss a beat. "Of course!" "Certainly. We'll be glad to have him."

"Now it wouldn't be charity," Frank added quickly. "Warren has some money set aside for winter, and he'd want to pay you for room and board."

"I won't stay with you unless you let me help out with the money," Warren said. "You know, I told Mom and Frank I could just stay here, at least until the house is sold. But I guess I've been outvoted."

"You'd be staying in an empty house with no furniture!" Betsy protested. "And anyhow, Warren, you've never shown much of a knack for cooking for yourself."

"No, no," Dasie's mother said, "this is the right solution. Really, Warren, it is. We'd love to have you. You can have Sam's old room."

Dasie felt a rising surge of anger. Sam's room! And what was she, wallpaper? All through the conversation—in fact, all through dinner—they'd gone on as though she wasn't even there. She felt the heat of fury redden her cheeks, numb her speech.

She rose, picked up her plate and Warren's to the left, and took them to the kitchen. She set the plates on the drain board, found her jacket among the pile on the chest freezer in the back hall, and walked out the door, along the driveway, and down the street toward home.

Dasie flung herself on her bed. Then as an afterthought she got up, called for Tattler, and, when he was in the room, slammed the door, hard, though there was no one there to hear it but herself.

She called Tattler up on the bed beside her, wrapped an arm around his shoulders, and buried her face in his neck. He heaved and moaned while the sound of Dasie's pounding heart filled her ears.

It was just a matter of waiting now. And the waiting didn't last so very long. Soon she heard the scuffle of footsteps in the kitchen followed by a sharp rap on her bedroom door, and then her mother stood in silhouette against the hall light.

"Dasie, how could you?"

Dasie didn't respond.

"Dasie? . . . I can't believe you'd do something so rude."

"Sorry," Dasie said. She couldn't believe her tongue worked. And she was only sorry about not thanking Aunt Betsy and Uncle Frank for dinner. That, she knew, was rude. The rest she wasn't sorry for.

"Dasie, you walked out without a word to anybody! How could you do that? Do you know how it made Warren feel? He thinks you're mad at him. We told him you're not, but he's pretty upset."

Dasie sat up. In the dark she looped a finger in Tattler's collar. "Warren's upset?" she said. "Does anybody care how *I* feel? Nobody talked to me. Nobody asked whether I wanted Warren to move in here."

"Well, Dasie, of course you do! We love Warren. We always have!"

"*You* love Warren," Dasie said. "You love him so much you'll let him have Sam's room. You love him so much you'll let him have Sam's *life*! What else are you going to give him? Tattler? Are you going to give him Sam's dog, too?"

"Dasie!"

"Warren's not my brother! Sam's my brother. Except you sent Sam away!"

"But you know what that's about. You know why, now more than ever. There's no life here for Sam!"

"There is too!" Dasie shouted. "There's enough of it to give away. Enough to give to Warren! We're staying in Grace Falls, and Warren is staying in Sam's life. But he can't have *me*, Mom. He can't be my brother. And he can't have Tattler!" She could feel Tattler tremble through his fur, but she did not let go.

For seconds—minutes?—her mother neither spoke nor moved. Then she said, "You're wrong about this, Dasie. Very, very wrong. I know you're upset about what's happening right now. We all are. But it's not Warren's fault, and you're wrong to take it out on him.

"We all need to help each other right now. That's what families are for. If we start fighting . . . well, we'll never make it. It's as simple as that." She turned from the door, closing it softly behind her.

The first big snow came on the twentieth of December. The flakes were wet and fat, and they fell on Dasie's hair and shoulders all morning as she helped Monica carry boxes from her room to the U-Haul parked in front of her house. Tattler was with her. Dasie took him everywhere now, except to school. By early afternoon the van was loaded, the car hitched to a trailer behind, and Monica and her parents climbed into the cab.

Dasie and Tattler stood there in the falling snow until the truck reached the end of Cedar Street, turned, and disappeared from sight. She turned back to Monica's house. The FOR SALE sign was tilted slightly to one side, and the windows were bare, vacant, absorbing the outside light into a dead interior. Dasie wanted, more than anything, to make one final dash to the door—to bang on it, walk in, and hear someone holler, "Monica, Dasie's here!"

Sam didn't make it home for Christmas. He bought a plane ticket, then twice changed his reservation. Up until Christmas Eve they all waited for the call telling them which flight he'd take into Faro. But the U.S. Navy had lost Sam's orders. He would stay in Chicago until they were found.

Dasie groped her way through a kind of fog, feeling as though the pieces of her life were just out of reach and slipping farther away. Only minutes after returning home from Christmas dinner at

Grandma Jenson's she could barely remember who sat where, who said what, what they ate. She was only sure that none of them had had a really good time.

For most of the next week Dasie's mother hardly left the house for fear of missing a call from Sam. There was still time. They might have a few days with him yet. But the phone never rang. Instead, on New Year's Eve, the postmistress called to say there was an Express Mail letter from Sam waiting at the post office.

Without so much as stopping to change her slippers for shoes, Dasie's mother grabbed her jacket and was out the door. When she took longer than expected to return, Dasie went to the window and saw her standing in the middle of the intersection, reading. She walked slowly home, dropped the opened letter on the kitchen table, and went to her room without a word.

> Dear folks,
>   Looks like I'll be on the U.S.S. Roosevelt, maybe going to the Adriatic Sea. That's the other way from you, so I cashed in my plane ticket and am sending the money to you enclosed. Please use it for something you need. I'll call when I get to Norfolk and come home on my next leave whenever that is.
>   Love, Sam

Dasie's mother stayed most of the day in her bedroom. When she came out, her face was pale and blotchy, her eyes swollen. Dasie's father put on his wool jacket and a ball cap and walked the money order down to the bank. He put it in Sam's savings account. "No way we're taking that boy's money," he said. "No way."

School reopened on the second of January and the next day let out early. The mill was closing that afternoon, and it was understood—just understood—that everyone would be there to hear the final whistle blow.

Dasie rode to the mill in her father's truck, her mother driving—she'd taken him to work that morning. In the parking lot they stood in a small sea of silent townspeople until two-thirty. Then came one long blast, *TWHOOOOOOOOOOO-oooooooooooooooooooooooooooooooo. . . .*

The sound pierced the ears and left a lingering echo, but somehow the silence that followed was louder; the whistle that had been a part of everyday life in Grace Falls for all of their lives would not be heard again.

In a minute men and women began to file out through the employee entrance past the time clock, and some through the cavernous loading bays. They wore hard hats and coveralls or scruffy lumber jackets with blue jeans. They carried lunch pails and gloves. None spoke nor lifted their eyes from the ground.

Dasie spotted Polly walking briskly toward the parking lot. As she craned her neck for her father, she realized the men coming through the loading bays weren't even punching out. Her father was among them, almost the last. He climbed into the driver's seat, handed his lunch bucket to Dasie, and stared straight ahead as he drove through the mill gate and along the road toward home.

Dasie never saw the road. She saw only her father's hands on the wheel, bulky and callused, cracked from the winter cold of the unheated mill.

At home he hung his hard hat on a hook inside the back door. He threw his coveralls in the laundry, then fished them out, and finally stalked out the back door around the garage to the garbage cans and came back without them.

CLAUDE: *This last three weeks Billy and I been working in timber no bigger than matchsticks out by Whistlepine Pass.*

PAT: *Where's that, Whistlepine Pass?*

BILLY: *You head out east and keep going to the end of the earth. Then you go eight more miles.*

DAVE: *Oh, yeah, I been there.*

BILLY: *Thursday last I filled one truck. Took one hundred ninety logs to make that one load.*

PAT: *A hundred and ninety logs to a load? That ain't timber! That's kindling.*

DAVE: *Way I see it, we got no business cutting timber that ain't half-growed when there's plenty of mature trees need cutting.*

BILLY: *Course there are. Every day we drive by mature stands with bug trees mixed in. Can't cut the bug trees for salvage, though. No, sir. Need a special permit for that. Time the permit comes through, bugs have spread so bad every tree in the stand is dead. They all fall on the ground and rot.*

CLAUDE: *Then they send us out to cut baby trees.*

PAT: *That's regulations now. Don't make no sense to me.*

BILLY: *That's 'cause you ain't no certified forester working for the U.S. government. Forester we got on this job ain't never been out to the site. Selects his trees sitting right there in the office.*

PAT: *Yeah, I heard of him. Young fellow with a good head of hair. Got a good-looking secretary helps him out.*

CLAUDE: *That's the one. Last year he let Johnson sidehill at a site out by Soda Mountain. Now there's nothing like sidehilling to devastate second growth. Way I see it, his brains all went for that hair.*

ten

Every morning Dasie's parents left for Morgantown before she left for school and returned after dark. The trip was taking twice the normal time; nearly every day another inch or two of snow fell on the roads. Dasie kept the fire going, adding a couple of small logs at lunchtime and more after school, opening the dampers so the house was toasty by the time her parents came in.

At night they seemed tired, but they spent part of each evening making a list of businesses to visit the next day. It paid off. By the end of the week her mother had found a job stocking shelves at a large variety store.

Her father wasn't so lucky, although he had a prospect—mounting tires at Wally's Wheels. If business picked up, they'd give him the job. "Wally says it's hard on the knees," he said. "But I told him I never was ambitious to have my parts last longer than I do. My knees are there to be used, same as everything else."

If her father got the job, the combined pay from both their jobs would be two dollars less an hour than her father had made at the mill. Not enough to pay for the health insurance they no longer had.

It seemed that every day someone else up and moved away from Grace Falls. There were two or three FOR SALE signs on every block, and talk grew worried. Who would buy all these houses? With no work in Grace Falls, who would come?

Aunt Betsy and Uncle Frank left on a bright frigid morning, a day done up in winter white and green under a brilliant sky. Warren went with them, following in his truck, and would return as soon as they were settled. He'd moved his few possessions the day before. Four boxes of clothes, two suitcases, his stereo, a carton of mechanics magazines and well-thumbed Bailey's catalogs, and a massive new motorcycle helmet, red-and-white, a Christmas gift from Betsy and Frank, were all piled on Sam's bed. He hung his fire helmet and turnouts on new nails in the utility closet.

His chain saw and gas can now sat alongside Dasie's father's in the garage. And the Harley, restored to mint condition—save for the new seat, which remained wrapped in clear plastic off to one side—was parked in the middle of the floor, protected by an oasis of space.

Dasie couldn't look in Sam's room. She stayed

busy in her own while Warren moved in. She was glad for the days he would be in Portland. Her parents had made it clear that no matter what her feelings, she was to welcome him. She hadn't figured out how.

There were now three empty desks in Mrs. Gower's class. And they stayed that way, empty. Dasie half expected someone to ask to change seats, but no one did. And she was glad. She didn't want to turn around and find someone else in Monica's place.

Dasie seldom finished all her homework assignments anymore. She rarely finished any of them. But then, neither did anyone else. And Mrs. Gower no longer seemed to care. The list of assignments she wrote on the board each morning had shrunk from six to one or two, and she no longer collected work personally. Instead you could just leave it in a yellow plastic bin on the windowsill.

It wasn't so much that Mrs. Gower stopped caring how they did as that she now cared more about how they *were*. At eleven o'clock each day she pulled her chair from behind her desk and sat right among them. "What's new?" she'd ask. Or, "How many of you saw the GOING OUT OF BUSINESS sign at the hardware store?" And soon they'd be talking.

There was always something to talk about. Becky's father was losing his job at the gas station, and she didn't understand what that had to do with the mill. Lyle wanted to know what was the difference between unemployment and welfare, and should you be ashamed if your family was on unemployment because so far neither of his parents had found work.

Many of the kids, Dasie included, said their parents weren't talking to them much—they were too wrapped up in their own problems. And Darlene said that lately it seemed all her parents did was yell at each other and at her.

There were questions about the school board and when they'd decide about the Grace Falls schools. Jessie was worried about what would happen if she was at school in Morgantown and got sick, really sick—would the bus bring her home?

They shared their problems with Mrs. Gower . . . and she shared hers with them. If the Grace Falls schools closed, she could go to work in another school in the country. But she didn't want to move from her home in Grace Falls, and she felt she was too old to commute over great distances on winter roads. So she might just retire. Except, she said, "I'd miss teaching. I'd miss it very much."

Dasie grew ashamed of her earlier dislike of Mrs. Gower. She no longer seemed like a grizzled drill sergeant, intent on spoiling their fun. Instead she seemed like one of them, a person with problems much like their own.

On the day Warren was due back from Portland, snow began to fall. The first flakes melted as they hit the ground, but the temperature soon dropped, and by early afternoon several inches lay on the roads. When Warren called from a rest stop, Dasie's dad shouted into the phone over a poor connection. "I think you should stop somewhere, son. Get a room for the night! The road between here and Morgantown is a sheet of ice covered by snow."

But Warren would make no promises. He wanted to be home, and anyhow he'd heard the storm could last for days. He said he'd drive carefully and telephone if he stopped.

The snow fell relentlessly and straight down. Each time Dasie went to the window there was less to see. A fuzzy coat of white blurred the details of everything in sight. Her mother, expecting the electricity to fail, got out the candles and oil lamps and set a kettle of seventeen-bean soup on the woodstove. Every few minutes Dasie heard a soft *whoosh* . . . and a thump as snow slid from one or another part of the metal roof. As time passed, her mother's conviction deepened, and she added pork rinds and onions to the soup.

Darkness came early, and Dasie stood at the window for minutes at a time, watching the steady fall of snowflakes past the streetlight on the corner. Her father turned on the scanner and paced as he listened to the stream of weather reports and travel advisories. Chains were now required on the road from Morgantown. "I hope to God Warren stops somewhere," he said.

Snow fell on through the evening. Tattler had to be coaxed out the door after supper, but once in the yard tore crazily, headlong through the snow.

Dasie watched, remembering how Sam used to go out and pelt snowballs at him until Tattler, frustrated, would fling himself hard enough to knock Sam down.

By eight in the evening there was still no word from Warren. Dasie's father put on a wool jacket and broad-brimmed hat and shoveled a path from the back porch to the gate. Then he took a broom to the snow on his truck and drove off to the fire hall, joining the crew clearing snow from the hydrants around town.

For a while Dasie and her mother listened to the radio scanner. The fire crew was shorthanded, and those who remained split the assignments of the firefighters who had moved or were away. Only one lane of the interstate remained open, and the roads from Faro through to Morgantown and Grace Falls were closed. Minutes after this last report, the lights flickered and died, and the scanner fell silent.

They lit the candles and oil lamps and waited in the warm wavering light for Dasie's father. The only sound now was the *whoosh* . . . of snow from the roof and the soft popping of the woodstove. Another hour passed before he returned, stomping snow from his boots onto the back porch. He hung his jacket over a chair backed up beside the stove, and soon the smell of warm, wet wool filled the air. There was still no word from Warren.

The clock ticked. At midnight, no longer able to keep her eyes open, Dasie went to bed, leaving her bedroom door ajar. She slept fitfully at first, aware of hushed and urgent conversation between her parents. But she was in a deep, sound sleep when the slamming of the back door and heavy footsteps in the kitchen burrowed into her consciousness.

She heard Warren's voice and her parents' and exclamations followed by laughter, then Warren's voice again: "Said the same thing to the CHP officer at the stop just out of Morgantown . . . 'I have an old uncle at home in Grace Falls. I need to get there.'"

"Old! The hell. Speak for yourself!"

Warren laughed. "Well, I think they were just looking for an excuse to let me through. They could see I was chained up and knew the road. But I'll tell you, knowing the road wasn't always a help. Times I drove fifteen miles an hour through an endless tunnel of white. Seems like the snow just keeps rushing at you, and that's all you can see."

"Well, you're here now, that's the important thing," Dasie's father said. "And you'd better get some sleep, because I'll tell you, if this keeps up, the department's going to need every hand we can get."

The oil lamp on the kitchen table cast a faint orange light down the hall to Dasie's room. She sat up just enough to make out the shape of Tattler on the end of her bed, head up, ears pricked. Dasie gave him a pat, then turned and pulled the covers over her ears. A part of her was glad Warren was back safe, but another part was still too angry to tell him so.

* * *

The storm lasted for three more days. They were days filled with effort. Twice the electricity came back on only to fail again within hours. Cooking, hot water, and clothes drying all depended on the woodstove. And outside the snow just kept piling up. Warren and Dasie's father were gone from dawn to dusk, clearing fire hydrants and responding to calls from senior citizens trapped in their homes, those no longer strong enough to shovel through the deep, wet snow outside their doors or the berms left by the town plow.

In spite of the constant work, there was something festive about those days, as though they'd all been given a holiday from worrying about anything except snow. And snow was one thing they knew how to handle.

By the fourth morning the roads were open, and Dasie's parents left early for Morgantown. Dasie dressed for school in the watery blue sunlight that filtered through the snow piled outside her window, then made her way to the kitchen. Warren was sitting in her father's chair, bent over his boot laces. "Listen, don't worry about the stove," he said. "I've got it set to last a few hours, and I should be back before lunch."

Dasie reached for a cereal bowl from the cupboard. "Where are you going?" she asked.

"Just up to my folks' place. I don't think there's much chance anyone'll look at the house in this weather, but just in case, I thought I'd better clear the walks." He stood and took his jacket from a hook by the door. "I might start hauling some of that wood down here, too," he said. "It's not doing anybody any good up there."

"No, I guess not," Dasie said. She filled her cereal bowl and sat at the table.

Warren opened the door and whistled once through his teeth. "Tattler! Want to go for a ride?"

Dasie's head snapped up. "No!" she said. "Leave Tattler alone!"

"Leave him *alone*? Dasie, I'm not going to hurt him. I'm just taking him out for some exercise. He's been cooped up in this house for days!"

"I don't care," Dasie said. "He's not your dog, and you can't just waltz off with him anytime you feel like it."

Warren stood silently for several seconds, just looking at her. Then he closed the door quietly, unzipped his jacket, and sat down again.

"Do you want to tell me what's going on?" he asked.

"I just did," Dasie said. "Tattler's not your dog, that's what's going on." She picked up the milk carton and poured milk over her cereal.

"This isn't just about Tattler," Warren said. "I mean, okay, fine, I won't take Tattler out if you don't want me to. But, Dasie, you've hardly spoken to me since I got here. I can't read your mind, you know. If I've done something, you need to tell me."

Dasie jabbed around in her cereal bowl with her spoon, avoiding his gaze. "I just don't think you should go helping yourself to other people's things without asking," she said.

Warren ran his hands over his eyes. "Like Sam's room, you mean? Look, Dasie, I know you're not exactly thrilled that I'm living here. But it wasn't my idea. Besides which it's temporary. When work starts up again this spring, I should be able to afford an apartment of my own."

"And what about Amy?" Dasie said. "Is she temporary, too?"

"Amy? No, of course she's not temporary! At least I hope not. But what does Amy have to do with this?"

Dasie shoved her bowl back from her place. She'd lost her appetite.

"Dasie?"

"It has to do with helping yourself to Sam's girl the minute he leaves town, that's what!"

"Sam's girl! Is *that* what you think?"

Dasie didn't answer. She picked up the bowl of uneaten cereal and carried it to the sink. Then she went to her room for her backpack and jacket.

When she got back to the kitchen, Warren was standing at the back door, blocking her way.

"Dasie, look at me. *Look!*" He was trembling, and his eyes were the same bright watery blue as the snow outside her bedroom window. "Do you really believe I'd ever, ever do one thing to hurt Sam? There's nothing, there's nobody . . . Amy was *never* Sam's girl! If she was, there's no way—" He broke off and shook his head. "Jeez, Dasie, if that's what you think, you don't know me at all." He turned on his heel and walked out the door, leaving it open behind him.

All morning in class Dasie hardly heard a word Mrs. Gower spoke. Her thoughts spun in circles. Was it possible she'd been wrong about Sam and Amy? How could that be? Didn't everyone think of them as a couple? If not a couple, at least a pair? Or was she the only one? Well, Monica had, for sure. So it couldn't have been just Dasie's imagination.

Still, she kept seeing Warren's stricken face and hearing him: "*Never* Sam's girl. . . . There's no way." It wasn't that she wanted to believe him. She didn't. And yet, somehow she was sure he'd spoken the truth.

She didn't understand, though. How could she have been so wrong? And what about Monica? Well, however it had happened, she'd made a mistake. A giant mistake. And worse, Dasie knew by noon, she'd been awful to Warren.

The house was warm at lunchtime, the stove freshly stoked, but there was no sign of him. She stood by the kitchen window as she ate her sandwich, but he never arrived. He wasn't there at the end of school either, and by the time she heard his truck, near four o'clock, she'd made and forgotten a dozen speeches.

He didn't come inside, and when several minutes had passed, Dasie went looking for him. She found him in the garage, socket wrench in hand, fitting the new seat to his Harley.

"Warren?"

"Yeah." He didn't turn around.

"I just wanted to say . . . to apologize. I mean, all this time I've been thinking . . ."

"Yeah, I know what you thought."

Dasie felt herself flush. "Well, I am sorry. I guess I've been pretty much of a brat lately."

"Forget it," Warren said. "It's over."

Dasie stood there behind him, uncertain, feeling she should say more but not knowing what. Finally she said, "If you want to take Tattler sometime, you can. It's okay with me."

He turned and looked at her, a quick, piercing look, then turned away, and Dasie knew at that moment how deeply she'd wounded him. "Yeah, okay," he said. "Thanks."

After that Warren wasn't around much except at dinnertime. He kept the house warm during the day and the wood box full, and sometimes Dasie came in at lunch to find the washer running but Warren gone. He never did take Tattler with him.

Often Dasie saw his truck parked up at the Ware house. Polly and Amy had found an apartment in Faro and were packing to move at the end of Amy's semester break. Dasie's father said it was a good thing they weren't trying to sell their house, because not a single one in Grace Falls had sold.

The phone rang on an early evening near the end of the month. Dasie's mother was barefoot at the counter, slicing carrots into the salad bowl, while her father manned a bubbling pot of spaghetti. Dasie was stirring wet food into Tattler's bowl of kibble. Warren, his fist full of forks and spoons, went for the phone. A moment later he stood in the kitchen doorway.

"Hank, it's for you," he said. "A man named Wilson from Consolidated Timber?"

They all stopped what they were doing and listened to his end of the conversation—which was sparse. "Uh-huh," he said. "Uh-huh . . . uh-huh . . . Yes, I am. . . . Yes. Uh-huh . . . uh-huh . . . I see. Yes, I see. Well, let me talk to my wife and get back to you. . . . Yes, I understand. . . . No, that's fine. . . . Yes, within a day or two."

He set the receiver in its cradle and turned to them with a slightly cocked smile. "I'll be damned," he said.

"What?" Dasie and her mother said at once.

"They're looking to hire a watchman at the mill, and they just offered the job to me." He ran a hand through his hair as his smile spread.

Dasie's mother sucked in her breath. "You're joking!" she said.

"No. They've still got logs and lumber sitting up there unsold yet. Not to mention a couple of million dollars in equipment to either auction or keep in mothballs. Guess they just figured out it's worth having some watchmen."

"Would this be permanent?" she asked.

"Indefinite, Wilson says. But, hey, everything's

indefinite. Wally's Wheels is indefinite. Once the snow season is past, they may not need me, and then I'd be right back where I started. At least Consolidated Timber will pay benefits. I'll have my health insurance and pension back." There was a light in his eyes that Dasie hadn't seen for weeks.

She felt giddy, almost woozy, as though she'd just made a tight turn on skates. "Then it'll be just like before!" she said.

"Not quite," her father said. "In the first place I'd be on the graveyard shift—Horace Perkins's old slot. I guess they offered it back to him, but he wasn't interested. Then the work, it'd be different." His smile dimmed for a second, then brightened again. He turned to his wife. "But you can quit that job now."

"Whoa!" she said. "Not so fast. I'm not quitting my job. It just so happens I like it."

"You do not," Dasie put in. "You complain all the time how your feet hurt." Not that she'd been asked, but she wished her mother would stay home again.

"I don't want my wife driving to Morgantown to work when it's not necessary," her father said. "What if something happened to you?"

Her mother set down the knife and folded her arms. She looked from Dasie to Hank with narrowed eyes. "Now see here—what if something happened to *you*, Hank Jenson? Do you know, every year I get more and more scared of that? And every year I've been more and more sure that if anything did happen, we'd all starve, 'cause I'd never be able to find a job. Because I'm getting older and older, and I don't know how to do anything!"

"But that's—," began Dasie's father.

"Just hush and listen to me!" she said. "I was scared to death to go looking for work. I was so sure I'd fail. But I didn't fail! And maybe it's not much of a job I got, but it's a start. And I already got my first paycheck!

"Do you know this is the first time in years I haven't been completely terrified every time the pager goes off for a routine flue fire, wondering who would take care of us if you got hurt?"

"But nothing's going to happen."

"No! You can't say that! You don't know! Anyway, it's too late to talk me out of this job, Hank. This isn't your decision, it's mine."

Dasie looked back and forth between her parents. Her mother had a locked-down expression, and her father . . . well, he just looked surprised. Warren leaned against the refrigerator with a faraway gaze, as though his mind were somewhere else.

Dasie's father shook his head, then walked across to his wife and put his arms around her. "Okay," he said. "You do what you want. Just so you understand we don't strictly need the money."

"If we don't strictly need it, then it'll go in the bank," she said.

"And you'll be real careful driving?" he asked.

She smiled. "Of course I will. Promise. And you'll stay off the tops of log decks, right?"

"Well . . . ," he said. They both laughed.

Dasie was disappointed at first. She'd always liked having her mother home. And with Sam and Monica gone, and Warren out so much, she often had an empty feeling.

But there was a shift in her parents' mood that night. At the dinner table they seemed more like their old selves, more relaxed. When they asked her how things were at school, she knew that this time they did not need her just to say, "Fine."

She told them what Mrs. Gower said—that it now seemed certain the Grace Falls schools would close at the end of the year. Everybody hated, just hated, the thought of being bused to Morgantown.

"It's gonna take some getting used to," her father said. "I guess I've been hoping for years both you and Sam'd be graduated before this happened."

"Well, it's another good reason for me to keep my job in Morgantown," her mother said. "I can drive you most days, and I'll be nearby if you need me."

Dasie never really noticed how quiet Warren had been until her father spoke up. "Warren, you haven't said much tonight. Anything wrong?"

Warren looked startled. "No," he said. "Just glad to hear about your job, that's all."

It had a hollow sound, and Dasie knew right away it wasn't true.

"Warren . . . ," her father said.

Warren traced the edge of his empty plate with his fork. For a long time he didn't answer. Then he said, "Heard today Johnson Logging's going down."

"Oh, Warren!" said Dasie's mother.

"I heard that over in Morgantown this week," Dasie's dad said. "Just didn't know whether you'd been told."

"Well, I stopped by Early's today, and he told me. Don't know whether Johnson was going to bother to let me know or not. Probably he'd just wait till I called him when the snow melts."

"What will you do?" Dasie asked.

Warren shrugged. "Don't know. Guess I'll start talking around and see if I can get on with one of the bigger outfits come spring."

Dasie's father folded his napkin and laid it carefully beside his plate. "Have you checked in over at the high school about the G.E.D. exam?" he asked.

"No," Warren said. "Not yet."

"You might do that soon," he said.

"Yes," Warren said. "Yes, I will."

But Dasie noticed that while his mouth said yes, his head was wagging no.

CURLY: *What's that Marv's got squirming in his pockets?*

PAT: *Brush-rabbit babies. Two of 'em. Cute little buggers, too.*

MARV: *Yeah, and my wife's gonna kill me. She just got done raising a pair last year. But, hell, I couldn't leave them there to die, now could I?*

CURLY: *I reckon not. But if she won't keep 'em, bring 'em by my place. My wife's still nursing that grey squirrel I brought in last month. We'll just add 'em in. Don't tell her you're coming, though. Just show up. If she sees 'em, she won't say no.*

MARV: *These'll keep her busy. They've been waiting two days for their mama without food. They're good and hungry, I'll tell you that.*

PAT: *What happened to the mama, you know?*

MARV: *Owls, I expect. There's a couple of pair making a good living off that section. Not that you'll meet a biologist can find one.*

CURLY: *Joe's the one whose wife is gonna kill him. He keeps picking up scorpions. Puts 'em in his lunch pail. Forgets to tell her.*

PAT: *I figure scorpions to be prehistoric. They can survive anything. Worked a burn last year where the fire went through so hot it* melted the rocks on the ground. Killed every living thing in its path. Except the scorpions. You pop the bark off some of those trees, and scorpions crawling around in there like you wouldn't believe.

CURLY: Yeah, that's how Joe found some of his. Don't know why he's so partial to scorpions. But his wife said the next time she opens his lunch box and finds scorpions in it, she's putting 'em in his sandwich the next day.

eleven

It wasn't the same. And that, Dasie supposed, was what she'd expected—that her father would return to the mill and everything would be the same. But there was nothing familiar about the night watchman's job, unless you counted location. "At least they didn't move the mill," her father said.

He left for work at midnight and came home to bed in the morning. He woke in time for supper, and Dasie's mother, uncertain what to do, cooked bacon, eggs, and pancakes one night, and meat loaf, potatoes, and gravy the next.

Dasie missed most the smell of sawdust and grease on his clothes. He came home as clean as he left, smelling only of cold air.

When he'd been there three weeks, he said, "If I'd known it would be like this, I don't know as I'd have jumped so quick. It's a ghost mill.

"You can't believe . . . to walk through those buildings so quiet you can hear a pin drop. I keep expecting any minute to hear the whistle blow. Other times for just a second I can see it all running again, hear the screech of the saws and the crash of lumber. Then I'll turn around, and there'll be the guys pulling chain."

He shook his head. "I can't decide what's worse, being up there alone or the fact I don't really work anymore. I just walk around. Doesn't seem like work to just walk around and look at a place where work used to be."

In the evenings after supper Dasie washed dishes while her parents sprawled on the living-room sofa and watched TV. This surprised her at first. They'd never been big on TV. Then she realized the point wasn't the TV, the point was spending time together. It was never long before her mother fell asleep, her head in her husband's lap. Later she'd wake just long enough to find her way to bed.

The fire department held a good-bye party for Polly Ware just before she and Amy moved to Faro. Dasie half expected they'd see more of Warren after Amy left, but instead it seemed he was gone most of every day. In the evenings he sometimes spent an hour or so in the garage, tinkering with the Harley. Dasie could hear it as she washed the dishes. He'd get it running for a while, then she'd hear it sputter and die.

Some evenings Warren watched TV with her parents, one leg flopped over the side of the armchair, but more and more often he went to Sam's room—*his* room—right after dinner and stayed there. He was studying, her mother said, though Dasie suspected the real reason had to do with her.

Warren spent the first weekend of February in Faro, and after that he seemed more remote than ever. It was as though he'd begun to fade. A kind of sadness clung to him, the way the night cold clung to her father's wool jacket.

He grew cautious, almost formal, asking before he'd take a soft drink from the refrigerator, apologizing if he left his boots by a chair. In all the years he'd been a visitor at their house, he'd always behaved as though he lived there. Now that he lived there, he behaved like a visitor. Dasie knew this was her fault. She'd made him feel like an intruder, something her parents and Sam had never done.

In her mind, she went over and over her argument with him. She wished she'd never said the things she said. If only she'd kept her thoughts to herself. She could have written to Sam. That would have been better. Well, she *did* write to him in a way—not coming right out and asking if he knew about Warren and Amy, but hinting. He hadn't answered, though.

And then it came back to her, like a remnant from a forgotten dream. The post-office lobby, the heat, a postcard from Sam she'd stuck somewhere. Her jacket. She went to her closet and pulled out her heavy down jacket. Sizes too big, and warmer than she needed, she rarely wore it. She rummaged deep in the pockets. Everything was in there. Wads of Kleenex, grocery lists, a school notice folded and forgotten, pencils. And the card.

Dear Dasie,
     Thanks for the letter. Glad to hear about the swans, wish I'd been there. Everyone here is sick with one thing or another me included. Too many people crammed together!
                                        Love, Sam

p.s. Think Amy's too busy w/ Warren to write.

Dasie sank to her bed and stared at the card. If only she'd read it before. If only Sam had *been* here.

As she watched Warren, and as the days passed, she knew she needed to find a way to repair the harm she'd done. She looked for a moment to catch him alone, and finally on a Thursday night, when he went out to the garage after supper, she folded the dishcloth over the spigot and followed him.

When she opened the garage door, he was sitting astride the Harley in a pool of light from the shaded overhead bulb. His arms were stretched full to the handlebars, and his head hung limp between his shoulders.

"Warren?"

His head snapped up. "Dasie! I didn't hear you come in."

"Could we talk?" she asked.

"Talk? Sure." He looked . . . disoriented, like

someone who'd just been wakened from sleep. "Sure, if you want. What's up?"

She stepped forward to the edge of the circle of light. "I just want you to know I really am sorry. I know I was horrible to you about Amy. I don't even know why I did that, Warren, honest I don't. I keep thinking about it, and it seems like maybe it was something I just wanted to be true—Sam and Amy—so in my mind I made it real.

"But mostly"—she looked at her feet and up again—"mostly I think I've been mad that Sam had to leave, mad without even knowing it, if you can understand that."

Warren's look was troubled, as though seeing her across a wide divide. He stared. Then blinked. Then stared.

"Besides," she said, "Tattler isn't my dog. He's not for me to choose about. He's Sam's. And Sam wouldn't want him cooped up all the time." Dasie felt a sudden sting of tears and bit her lip. "I want things to be the way they used to be, Warren. The way they were when Sam was here and we were friends."

Warren's eyes softened and gathered focus. He drew a deep breath and cocked his head. "We're still friends, Dasie," he said gently. "We'll always be friends."

"But not like we used to be, Warren. We hardly talk. We don't joke around. And I know it's my fault, but I don't know how to fix it."

"Oh, Dasie, Dasie, is that what you think? That I'm mad at you?"

"Well, we . . ."

"Because I'm not," Warren said. "This isn't about you, Dasie. I've got things on my mind, that's all."

Maybe it was the way the overhead light cast shadows all down his face, but Dasie was suddenly sure she'd never seen anyone look more sad. And she didn't understand. Didn't understand and didn't know how to help.

"You want to go for a ride?" he asked suddenly.

"A ride? You mean now? On the *Harley*?"

"Sure," Warren said. "That's what I was doing when you came in. I was on a long ride. Come on. Climb on up here behind me."

Dasie moved cautiously forward. The Harley was so big up close. She took a deep breath and threw a leg over the saddle behind Warren.

"Now put your arms around my waist," he said. "Tight. That's it. Ready?"

"Ready," Dasie said.

"Now close your eyes," Warren said.

Dasie did.

"The first thing you need to know when you go on a ride is where you're going. Do you know where you're going, Dasie?"

"No," she said.

"Me neither. That's the trouble." He laughed a gentle, rueful laugh, then went on. "The next thing is you need to be able to see the road. Can you see it?"

"Not with my eyes shut!" Dasie answered.

"Yeah. That's another trouble. Except my trouble is worse than yours, because I can't see the road even with my eyes open."

Dasie loosened her grip and pulled away.

"No, hang on," Warren said. "This is important, Dasie. Trust me, okay?"

Dasie sat still for a moment, considering. Then she put her arms back around Warren. Her hands barely met, and this time she leaned one cheek against his back. She could hear his heart thump, strong and steady, and now she heard his words from the inside.

"You see, Dasie, if you know where you're going, if you keep your eyes open and can see the road, then you'll know just how to take the turns. It's instinct. The turns come, and you lean into them, this way or that way. It's easy then." As he spoke he leaned a little left and then a little right so Dasie began to feel she was on a real ride.

"That's the great thing about Hank and Anne," he said. "They see the turns, and they lean into them. Your folks have always been my heroes, Dasie. I've always wanted to be just like them.

"Except if you're me ... well, if you're me, you're maybe bullheaded. And maybe blind, too.

"All my life, Dasie, I only wanted to go one place. Everyone said, 'You can't go there! There's no such place anymore!' But I had my mind made up, and I was going. No matter what anyone said, I was going!

"Only now I found out there really is no such place anymore." He stopped the gentle sway of the imaginary ride and the thump of his heart grew faster. Dasie loosened her grip again, and this time climbed down. There was something in his voice that scared her. She stuck the tip of her thumb in her mouth and studied his face. It was ashen, his eyes hollow. It seemed he had run out of words, that he'd withdrawn beyond Dasie's reach.

"What's wrong, Warren? Please, you have to tell me what's wrong."

He shook his head, and for a minute, maybe two, she thought he wouldn't answer. At last he said, "I can't find a job for the spring. There's no work for any cutters with less than fifteen years' experience. Not anywhere near here. Not anywhere in this *state*, Dasie. All the small logging outfits are folding. The closest I could get work is maybe Alaska. But they're clear-cutting up there. I mean, even if I didn't mind going to Alaska, which I do, do you know what it means to clear-cut? It's not a job for a logger who takes pride in his work."

"Butchers," Dasie whispered. She could hear her father say it.

Warren nodded. "So now I'm supposed to do what? I promised Mom I'd get my G.E.D. She gave me my father's bike on that promise." He ran his fingers along the bright chrome handlebar. "But I can't do it, Dasie. I can't do it because I never was any good at school, and I can't think of a single thing I want to do with a college education. And I don't know whether that's just me being bullheaded again, or if it means there really isn't anything for me but logging. All I know is I've been letting folks down for most of my life, and I'm about to do it again."

"You're not letting me down," Dasie said.

"No," he said. "No, I suppose I'm not. I'm glad for that, Dasie."

He was quiet again for a minute, then said, "Right now I'm looking at selling this Harley just to live for the next year. But then what?

"Amy thinks I should move to Faro and go to community college with her. Get a job in a gas station to pay my way. But see, Amy wouldn't mind that, because she knows what she wants, and college is how to get there. Me, all I see is destinations for someone else. I can't find my road, Dasie, even with my eyes wide open."

Dasie wasn't aware of tears on her cheeks until a wintry draft turned them cold. Then she leaned forward and put her arms around Warren's neck. He never loosened his grip on the handlebars. But she felt his head tilt slightly to one side, just enough to lean against hers.

Snow fell on and off all the next day. It was Valentine's Day, and when Dasie got home from school, she found the note from Warren propped against the saltshaker on the kitchen table.

Gone to Faro. Back late. Tattler's with me.
—W.

Dasie's mother was fretful that night. "He picked some fine weather for driving to Faro," she said.

"We can call Polly and make sure he got there," her father said. "But Warren knows how to drive these roads in the snow, and he doesn't care to be hovered over. Anyhow, this storm isn't expected to amount to more than a few inches."

Her mother sighed. "Warren just worries me, that's all. He's got a deep vein of something I don't really understand, and I swear he never leaves this house without me wondering if I'll ever see him again."

"He's got Tattler with him," Dasie said. "Warren won't let anything happen to Sam's dog." As she said it, she knew it was a truth they could count on. If it weren't for Tattler, maybe she'd worry, too.

She went to bed not long after her mother did and stirred only a little when her father left for work. How long she slept, she didn't know. And she couldn't say what woke her. But she sat up suddenly in the dark with a feeling of urgency.

Outside her windows the sky was breaking, and a full, ringed moon peeked through the clouds. Her father had been right about the storm. She fumbled in the dark for her slippers and a sweater.

When she opened her door, the light was still on over the kitchen stove. She walked past the table toward the back door and all but fell over Tattler. He was standing quietly, tail thumping.

Tattler. She ran her hand through his ruff. So Warren was back. She turned toward his bedroom, and that's when she heard it. Somewhere outside, a chain saw.

Who would run a chain saw in the middle of the night? Dasie opened the back door and stepped out onto the porch. She could hear it more clearly now. In the still, snow-muffled night it was the only sound, a deep whine that seemed to move with the clouds. Only it was farther away than she thought. And it wasn't a chain saw. Not even close. It was a motorcycle.

Dasie's heart was suddenly racing. In the bright light of the moon she saw the footprints through the snow. Tattler's and Warren's to the back door, and Warren's again, alone, toward the garage. With Tattler on her heels she ran down the steps, following Warren's footprints to where they ended at the side door to the garage. Then she ran around to the front. A lone tire track ran to the street.

At the end of the drive she stopped and listened again. *BBWHAPPPHHHH . . . bbwhappphhhh.* The engine shifted up, then shifted down. She could almost see him in her mind's eye as he slowed to make a turn, speeded up again for the length of a block, then slowed again.

What was he doing out there? What was he doing riding that bike through town in the middle of a snowy night? Dasie turned a complete circle, heading first for the house to wake her mother, then back toward the road, where maybe she should wait for Warren, stop him if he came by.

She cocked her head and listened, trying to place exactly where he was. The engine slowed for a minute, sputtering at an idle, then suddenly revved again, moving up through the gears, higher and higher. He was out on the highway. He was on the highway headed east, and gaining speed.

She turned and bolted for the house. But just as she reached the porch, it stopped. The noise stopped. It didn't wind down; it didn't fade away. It just stopped.

Dasie froze, knowing what it meant, knowing with a *certainty* what it meant, but at the same time refusing to know. *It can't be. No. It can't. It cannot be.* Then Tattler raised his head and howled, a long bone-chilling howl. He did it again. And yet once again, until there came from Dasie a cry louder still. *"Warren! WARREN. . . ."*

twelve

They found Warren's helmet on Sam's dresser, where it had sat since he moved in. On Sunday morning, with Betsy and Frank expected by early afternoon, Dasie's father tossed it in the bed of his pickup, loaded his chain saw and gas can, and drove up to the highway.

He cut the tree down. And nobody stopped him. The man who had never wasted a stick of timber in his life cut down a ninety-foot-tall, thirty-inch-diameter ponderosa pine, bucked it into one-foot lengths, and kicked the pieces down over the embankment. He wasn't going to leave it there for Betsy to see—for any of them to see—scarred by the impact of the Harley and Warren's body.

He stood in the snow, panting, covered in sawdust and sweat, and looked down into the ravine, where the tree lay in pieces. Then, with all his might, he hurled the helmet after it.

Betsy would not be told that Warren wasn't

wearing the helmet. She'd never be told anything except that the road was icy and—if she asked—that, yes, he'd been getting ready to take his G.E.D.

Sam was on his way home from the Adriatic Sea. It had taken some doing. Emergency leave could be given in the case of a death in the immediate family. A cousin was not considered immediate family. But after a long talk, his chief said, "As I understand it, Warren Jenson was your brother. That's what I'm writing on this form." And four hours later Sam was on a Navy plane bound for Sicily. From Rome he telephoned with his schedule to New York, saying to expect him on the first flight into Faro Monday morning.

Dasie was half-senseless, dazed at the awfulness of those days. There was nothing left in her that was strong or even wanted to be. The phone rang incessantly. There were visitors, arrangements to be made, a kind of busyness that got in the way of the one thing that mattered, that Warren was dead. And yet, in every lull she felt a thunderous crash of pain, an ache so huge, her only wish was to flee. Sometimes she found whole hours had passed that she couldn't account for. Other things seared so deeply, she lived them over and over.

Warren's footprints in the shallow snow lingered all through Saturday and Sunday. His footprints. As though she might follow them and find him at their end, standing in a circle of light.

It was impossible to open the back door without seeing his truck and believing that he'd just pulled up and would in a moment be visible at the gate. But time after time after time he did not come. Each time he didn't come, Dasie remembered afresh the reason why.

Her mother never stopped crying. She wept sometimes more and sometimes less, but she always wept, silent rivers of tears without end.

Her father carried a kind of anger, a coiled fury, she'd never seen before. He would not sit still. When there was nothing to be done, he went to the shed and with one heave tore down a whole rack of wood. He found reason to split large logs into smaller ones, then stack them again—fast!—as though chased by time.

The pager went off for a flue fire on Sunday night, and in the kitchen Dasie's father turned first one way, then another, a look of confusion on his face. He opened the utility closet door. As he reached inside, his knees buckled, and a cry escaped him, a sound Dasie understood as a deep and mortal wounding. With Warren's turnout jacket in his hands, he walked out into the night cold and was gone for hours. Somewhere. Not to the fire.

Polly and Amy had returned to Grace Falls Saturday night, and Polly offered to make the drive back to Faro to meet Sam. Dasie asked to go with her. She slept in her clothes on Sunday night, shoes and all, stretched carefully on her bed. She slept fitfully, dreamed, bolted awake, then slept and dreamed again. At four-thirty in the morning she got up and waited on the back porch for Polly.

When she climbed into the cab of the truck, Polly gave her a strong and lingering hug. "Are you okay?" she asked.

Dasie nodded, then shook her head. She snapped her seat belt in place and asked, "How's Amy?"

"Right now she's asleep on your grandma's couch. It's the first sleep she's had." Polly sighed. "She's having a hard time, though. Told me today she's been in love with Warren ever since she was in second grade. All those years of waiting for him to notice her. And now she thinks she should have saved him. It's rough."

Dasie swallowed hard. "I didn't know that," she said.

"None of us knew," Polly said. "Nobody but Sam, I guess. Amy always told him everything."

"Warren, too," Dasie said.

"Mmm. Warren, too. Sam was probably the only one who really knew Warren. At your grandma's house yesterday afternoon that's what everyone was saying. That Sam's the one who really knew him."

They drove the next hour in silence. Then, in the tiny Faro terminal building, they stood at the window, watching the runway as the sun came up. On time almost to the minute, the lights of the little twin-prop came into view. Soon it taxied to the yellow line outside the door and stopped.

It was a twenty-nine-seat plane, and this morning only eight passengers disembarked. Sam was the last. He carried a large green duffel and seemed not to be looking for anyone. As Dasie watched him walk across the tarmac, she had two opposing sensations: that she'd have known him anywhere and that she'd never have picked him out in a crowd. The wind caught the collar of his dress blues and flapped the cuffs of his pants. He was thinner than she remembered, tanned, and more . . . erect.

"Sam?"

"Dasie." He looked out of hollow eyes. No amount of tan and military bearing could disguise his plainly shattered heart.

"Good to see you, Polly," he said.

"You, too, Sam. We're parked right over here."

They drove home, through Faro and Morgantown and over the pass through snow-tipped trees that reached up and met in a sheltering embrace. In the warmth of the truck Dasie drew her first full breath since Warren's death. The "real cowboy," the one in the middle, fell asleep with Sam's arm around her shoulder.

Early that afternoon they followed the hearse through the cemetery gates. Sam, Dasie's dad, Uncle Frank, Martin Raines, Joe Early, and Danny Cabrini, who had returned for the funeral, carried Warren's casket from the back of the hearse to the freshly dug grave site alongside Uncle John's. It was true, Dasie saw through the snow: the rocks around Uncle John's grave had moved again.

As the minister read prayers, they clung to one another in unsteady groups of two or three—

Grandma Jenson, Dasie's father, Betsy, Frank, Sam, Dasie, her mother, Amy, and Polly—surrounded by a blur of friends and neighbors. The number of people caught Dasie off guard. As the minister spoke words not really soothing but unmistakably final, she remembered that the faces familiar to her had also been familiar to Warren. And his to them. Warren's death, a death in Grace Falls, was felt by everyone.

Dasie glanced only briefly at Aunt Betsy and Grandma Jenson. What they felt was so severe, so altering, that it was hard to recognize them for the people she'd known her whole life. She had to turn her eyes away.

An icy breeze knifed through her as the coffin was lowered into the ground. Sam, Uncle Frank, and her father each took a turn with a shovel, tossing earth into the gaping hole. It was a sound Dasie knew she would never forget—the rasp of the shovel and the splatter of earth onto polished wood.

After his turn, her father plunged the shovel into the piled dirt and turned and walked down the hill out of sight. A few minutes later other people began to exchange hugs and drift away. When her mom put a hand on Dasie's shoulder, she shook her head. "In a minute," she said.

Sam, his eyes red rimmed and his face grey beneath his tan, peeled off his peacoat and took up the shovel again.

"Sam," their mother said, "the grounds crew will do that."

"No!" he said with unexpected force. "This is *mine* to do for Warren. Nobody does this but me."

His voice sent a shock through Dasie. She turned and ran up the hill to the old cemetery and fell to her knees, panting, in front of Dasie's stone. She was sweating and shivering at the same time. *Asleep in the Arms of Angels.*

Was that where Warren was? Asleep in the arms of angels? She wished she could believe it, but she couldn't. Not yet. The only place she could imagine him asleep was curled on the sofa in their dining room, as she'd seen him for so many years of her childhood. But she wouldn't see him there again. And she wouldn't see him stuffing pancakes into his mouth at the kitchen table. And, years from now, she wouldn't see him dance at her wedding.

Warren wasn't asleep anywhere. He was dead in a box in the ground. And when night came, he would still be there, alone, cold beneath the earth. How could they just go home and leave him here?

Sometime later she heard footsteps behind her and Sam's voice, soft. "It's done now, Dasie. Time to go."

Dasie wiped her face across the sleeve of her coat. "I can't," she said.

"A minute more then," Sam said. He squatted beside her.

"I had a dream last night while I was waiting for you," Dasie said. "While your plane was in the air over Iowa or someplace. It was the most real dream I've ever had. We were all together, you and me, Mom and Dad and Warren. Even Tattler. Just like the night after the fire in the log yard, remember? We were all together, and we were so happy. And in the dream I just *knew* it was never going to change."

"But it *has* changed, Dasie."

"I know," she said. "I know that. But, Sam, it's changed so much. And it started right after the fire. First you left, and then the mill closed, and pretty soon it seemed like . . . like *Grace Falls* was leaving. Everyone and everything that used to be was just going away. And now Warren's left in the worst way of all. Because he can't come back. Ever."

"I know," Sam said. "It's like Dad always said. But worse. Worse because we never thought . . . Warren . . ." He turned to Dasie with tears streaming down his face. "And you're going to have to leave, too, Dasie. In just a few years, maybe sooner. You understand that, don't you? You need to leave Grace Falls and make a life for yourself. I've been putting money in the bank for you, so you can go to college no matter what happens. You have to do that. Say you'll do it, Dasie."

Dasie nodded. "Okay," she said, "I will."

"You won't just try to hang on? Promise me."

She shook her head. "No, I won't." Then she said, "But I will come back, Sam. I don't know exactly how yet, but I thought about it a lot these last three days. Our whole family's here, Sam. Even the ones who are dead. And it's a good place to be, Grace Falls. I know I could live somewhere else, but I want to come back here. Someday."

Sam rubbed the backs of his hands across his cheeks, then leaned forward and bumped her forehead with his. "That's a fine thing to want," he said.

Dasie sighed. She reached out and brushed the crust of snow off the top of baby Dasie's stone. "I've looked for her family," she said. "W. E. and A. C. Jenson. I haven't found them yet."

"You haven't?" Sam smiled. "But they're right there, Dasie." He pointed to a patch of snowy ground to the left.

"There's nothing there," Dasie said. "I've looked."

"Then look again come spring," he said. "There are two small flat squares of marble. The last time I was here, the sod was creeping up around the edges. They're probably grown over now, but you'll be able to find them if you scratch around a little."

Dasie blinked. "You've been here before?"

"Sure I have. Mom used to bring me every spring. We'd walk around and visit everyone. At the time, I didn't think there was anything strange about it. But now . . ."

"I know," Dasie said. "I think I could talk to the strangers. But Warren . . ." She looked back over the rise toward the new Jenson plot and her throat swelled.

"We should go now," Sam said. "We're not doing Warren any good here."

Dasie tried to move, but couldn't. "I didn't do him any good anywhere," she said. And she told Sam then the story of her anger, of her hardness to Warren, who had never done an unkind thing to anyone, who had only ever loved her.

Sam listened, his head down, hands folded. Then, when she was done, he said, "I know all about that, Dasie. But even if it had never happened, it wouldn't have changed anything.

"What happened to Warren wasn't because of you. And it wasn't because of Amy either, although right now she thinks it was. And it wasn't because of Dad, even though I know he blames himself. It probably wasn't even about Aunt Betsy and Uncle Frank, though I think they'll always feel like they failed him." He drew a deep breath. "And I suppose it wasn't even because of me," he said, "though part of me will always believe that if I'd been here, he'd never have taken that ride."

"Then what *was* it because of?" Dasie asked. There had to be something. Warren couldn't have died for no reason at all.

"Everything. Nothing. The times. Circumstances." Sam sighed and ran his hand across the glittering crust of snow in front of Dasie's stone. "In the end I guess it was about Grace Falls and Warren," he said. "I think that's what Warren would tell us if he could."

179

They walked down the hill in the twilight of a Grace Falls winter. Dasie held tight to Sam's hand, barely able to feel him with her frozen fingers. At the gate they stopped and looked up the hill.

"I'm coming back," Dasie said.

"Me, too," Sam said. "We can come back together."

EARLY'S SAW SHOP

CLOSED

NATALIE HONEYCUTT most recently published *Ask Me Something Easy*. Other novels include *Invisible Lissa, The All-New Jonah Twist, The Best-Laid Plans of Jonah Twist, Juliet Fisher and the Fool-proof Plan,* and *Josie's Beau.*

She and her family live in McCloud, California.